A VILLA IN SICILY:

VINO AND DEATH

(A Cats and Dogs Cozy Mystery—Book Three)

FIONA GRACE

Fiona Grace

Fiona Grace is author of the LACEY DOYLE COZY MYSTERY series, comprising nine books (and counting); of the TUSCAN VINEYARD COZY MYSTERY series, comprising six books (and counting); of the DUBIOUS WITCH COZY MYSTERY series, comprising three books (and counting); of the BEACHFRONT BAKERY COZY MYSTERY series, comprising six books (and counting); and of the CATS AND DOGS COZY MYSTERY series, comprising six books.

Fiona would love to hear from you, so please visit www.fionagraceauthor.com to receive free ebooks, hear the latest news, and stay in touch.

BOOKS BY FIONA GRACE

LACEY DOYLE COZY MYSTERY
MURDER IN THE MANOR (Book#1)
DEATH AND A DOG (Book #2)
CRIME IN THE CAFE (Book #3)
VEXED ON A VISIT (Book #4)
KILLED WITH A KISS (Book #5)
PERISHED BY A PAINTING (Book #6)
SILENCED BY A SPELL (Book #7)
FRAMED BY A FORGERY (Book #8)
CATASTROPHE IN A CLOISTER (Book #9)

TUSCAN VINEYARD COZY MYSTERY
AGED FOR MURDER (Book #1)
AGED FOR DEATH (Book #2)
AGED FOR MAYHEM (Book #3)
AGED FOR SEDUCTION (Book #4)
AGED FOR VENGEANCE (Book #5)
AGED FOR ACRIMONY (Book #6)

DUBIOUS WITCH COZY MYSTERY
SKEPTIC IN SALEM: AN EPISODE OF MURDER (Book #1)
SKEPTIC IN SALEM: AN EPISODE OF CRIME (Book #2)
SKEPTIC IN SALEM: AN EPISODE OF DEATH (Book #3)

BEACHFRONT BAKERY COZY MYSTERY
BEACHFRONT BAKERY: A KILLER CUPCAKE (Book #1)
BEACHFRONT BAKERY: A MURDEROUS MACARON (Book #2)
BEACHFRONT BAKERY: A PERILOUS CAKE POP (Book #3)
BEACHFRONT BAKERY: A DEADLY DANISH (Book #4)
BEACHFRONT BAKERY: A TREACHEROUS TART (Book #5)
BEACHFRONT BAKERY: A CALAMITOUS COOKIE (Book #6)

CATS AND DOGS COZY MYSTERY
A VILLA IN SICILY: OLIVE OIL AND MURDER (Book #1)

CHAPTER ONE

Getting ready for your hot date?

The phone buzzed as Audrey Smart was leaning forward, listening with her stethoscope to her patient's heartbeat.

She peered at the message from her sister and checked the time. Two hours and counting. This was her last appointment of the night, and then ... big things were about to happen. She could feel it. She shivered again at the thought.

"I don't know!" the female transplant from Canada said, wringing her hands and pacing the floor of the clinic. "He just looks so ... I don't know. Sad."

"Well," Audrey said, pulling the device from her ears. "He *is* a Basset Hound."

"Yes, but isn't there such a thing as... like, dog depression? Ever since I moved him out here, he's just looked *especially* glum. Are you sure he's not sick?"

"His vitals are all perfect. He's the picture of health. When did you get him?"

"Oh, Bubba was a graduation present from my boyfriend. In Toronto. I've had him since he was a puppy," the woman, Connie Wilkes, said.

"He's been through a lot, then, hmm?"

Connie tapped her chin. She'd gone through the whole story—how she'd purchased a one-euro home in Mussomeli, Sicily, a couple months ago, same as Audrey. She couldn't have been much more than twenty-five. Audrey had to give her props. It wasn't an undertaking for the faint of heart, that was for sure. "I suppose just about *everything* has changed for him. But I thought he would like it here. It's warmer, and he hates the snow. He gets to lie out on the patio and soak up the sun, which he loves. But other than that ... nothing."

Audrey smiled and petted the poor dog's droopy ears. "You know, dogs are just like us humans. They have good days and bad. And yes, they can be depressed. But let me ask you something. Have you been doing renovations on your place?"

1

She groaned and ran a hand through her long dark hair, making the charm bracelet on her wrist jingle. *"Have I!* Girl, I've been working twelve-hour days, getting my little corner of paradise into shape. I swear, I don't ever sleep anymore. I'm being run ragged!"

Same, Audrey thought, thinking of her own suffering little place. She'd been putting so much time into getting her veterinary business off the ground and successful, her renovations at home had taken a serious backseat. *So much the same.*

"It's a huge undertaking. You have to be stressed. And dogs can feel that. There's a strong correlation between a pet's disposition and his owner's. It's likely Bubba can feel how stressed out you are, and he is absorbing some of that stress," Audrey said as the dog flopped over on its side and gave her enormously sad eyes. "Not to mention that you've probably been so busy with renovations to pay him much attention?"

Connie sighed. "You might be right."

"Luckily, it doesn't take much to perk a dog up." Audrey reached into a cabinet and pulled out a tub of peanut butter. She scooped out a spoonful and held it up in front of Bubba.

Bubba's eyes immediately lit up and he jumped to his feet, licking the spoon clean.

Audrey smiled as he continued to run his tongue over it, looking for any spot he might have missed. "See? Sometimes the smallest little bit of attention you pay will work wonders. That's what makes them so lovable, right? They exist to please us. He probably felt bad you were feeling bad."

Connie smiled. "Aw. That's all?" She lifted him up into her arms and spoke in baby-talk, "Oh, baby, I'll make sure I don't ignore you anymore! What do you say to a nice, long walk to the park?"

Audrey opened the exam room door and led her patient and his owner out to reception. "Yes, I bet he'd love that. But if he does have any other complaints, just give me a call. I'm always here for you guys!"

"I will. Thanks so much!" she said, heading out the door.

Audrey tidied up the magazines in the empty reception area. The place was small, but neat, with modern lines and pictures of happy pets on the walls. The construction was complete, but it still smelled like paint. There was a pile of mail waiting for her—probably bills. She grabbed her letter opener from the reception desk and then set it down.

It'd been a long day of steady clients, almost since opening at nine. Now, the sun was setting, and she had places to be.

One place, actually. A very important place, or at least, she hoped. She hoped that what happened tonight would be something she remembered the rest of her life.

So the mail could wait until tomorrow. She flipped the sign on the door from *Aberto* to *Chiuso*. Then she went into the back to check on the latest batch of strays that had come in—a couple kittens and an older dog.

Talk about a sad dog. This was a mangy-looking mutt with matted fur, shaking in his cage. She went over to him and sighed as she petted him. "Oh, Bruno," she whispered to him. "Don't you worry. We'll get you fixed up with a new owner who'll take good care of you. Okay? What do you say about that?"

She looked around the crowded place, at all the sad faces staring back at her, hoping it was true. The back room was now filled with animals looking for a good home. Since the clinic had opened a month ago, word was definitely spreading about her practice, so the place was now busy from morning to night, and people from neighboring towns were starting to bring in their pets. And strays.

Lots of strays. If there was one thing the crumbling old town of Mussomeli, Sicily, had in spades, it was strays.

That's why the town had accepted her application for a one-euro house almost the second she'd sent it in. She'd been getting tired of her life in Boston, wanted to shake things up, and submitted the bid, never really expecting anything to happen. Then, a week later, she was on a flight across the Atlantic, to her new home.

And just in time, too. The stray population in the city was staggering. Though she kept finding new homes for them, more flooded in almost every day. Which reminded her, she had to set up that free spay-and-neuter clinic. There was hardly ever much of a vacancy at Hotel Smart, though she was proud that she and her vet center were playing a small part in eliminating the stray problem here.

But those sad faces ... sometimes Audrey wished she could take them all home with her.

Not that that could happen—her place might have been the biggest of the old, crumbling properties in Mussomeli, but right now, it was a giant pile of sawdust and broken plaster. A construction crime scene. She cringed at the thought of it as she filled water trays and made sure the animals had their cuddles. Then she waved them all goodbye sadly, as though she wouldn't see them again in another ten hours. She'd have to wait until her renovations were done before she could think of any more pets. "Goodbye, my loves!"

She stepped outside to see Nick, waiting dutifully for her.

"Hi, Nick!" she said to her little pet fox, who'd made it a habit of being out on the stoop every evening at six, to escort her home.

He darted between her legs, tickling her calves with his big, bushy tail. She bent down and stroked his chin. "All right, all right. Let's go home and get you some food. An apple? I think I have one at home."

He purred in answer.

She had to get there, and soon. She had to get ready for those big, life-changing things to happen.

*

Every time she came home to her place on Piazza Tre, knowing how far other one-euro home buyers were getting with their renovations, she felt a little squeezing in her chest. She had plans on top of plans to make her place the prized jewel of Mussomeli, but with her vet practice, no time at all.

So as she walked, she tried to ignore the sights of other homes in the midst of renovation. But it was pretty obvious, considering how narrow the streets were. One owner was painting his home a cheery pale pink that looked gorgeous. Someone else had gotten lovely new shutters, and yet another new homeowner was repairing the scrollwork on their balcony. She waved hello to everyone she passed, feeling a little jealous. She'd hate to be known as the American who owned the "Disaster of Piazza Tre."

Still, she loved the town. It had been a virtual ghost town a couple months ago, but now it was showing more signs of life as more and more units were sold. Though the cobblestone streets were full of crumbling buildings, Baroque-style architecture, and old-world charm, the place had a new, young energy zinging through it. A kind of electricity. She passed an old cobbler's and a farm market which was just closing up, pulling their wares off the sidewalk for the night. The owner, a mustached man who always called *Ciao* to her in the mornings, offered her a paper bag. She opened it.

"Oh, tomatoes!" she said with a smile as she peered in at the biggest, ripest fruits she'd ever seen. A perfect time to practice her Italian. "*Grazie.* How much do you want for them?"

4

He waved her away. "On the house! It's the least we can do for our lovely *Dottore*."

"*Grazie mille*, that's so kind," she told him in Italian, bursting with pride at her ability to carry on a conversation in the Italian language without tripping all over her tongue. As much as she cursed herself for mispronouncing just about everything, she was getting better at her comprehension.

She waved at him as she crossed the narrow, slanting street, already wondering what kind of dinner she could scrounge up. *Tomatoes and ... more tomatoes.* She'd meant to go to the market, but she'd been too busy. Her cupboard was as close to bare as it could get. Nick would be lucky to get that apple.

Tomorrow, I'll do the shopping. On the way home from work. I have to, she told herself, yawning at the mere thought. She'd been dining out every night at the local cafes and bistros, totally spoiling herself, because she'd been too tired to cook. Besides, she hated cooking.

When she rounded the corner onto her street, she smiled at the sight of who was standing on her front stoop, waiting for her.

"Oh, *Polpetto*!" she cried, rushing to the giant mastiff's side as it began to beat its tail like a drum against the side of the wall. Funny how a dog could always lift her spirits mile-high. She wrapped her arms around him and let him lick her face.

"Uh ... I'm here, too," a voice beside the dog said.

She rolled her eyes at her gorgeous neighbor, Mason. With his cinnamon hair falling in his face and his Led Zeppelin T-shirt nicely clinging to his defined pecs, she always had the urge to get giggly around him. "Yes, but you're not nearly as adorable."

"That is a matter of opinion," he muttered, smirking at her.

The giggle almost forced its way out, but luckily, beside her, Nick let out a hiss, and Polpetto, a rare bark. The two were not exactly best friends. "Calm down," she said to her fox, nudging him away as she shuffled her purse in her hands with the bag, trying to retrieve her keys. "What are you guys doing here?"

"Why're you acting so surprised? Haven't we been here every day this week to help you with your repairs?"

"I know. I just ..." *Thought I told you I had plans for tonight.* "Forget it. Come on in. I have ... tomatoes."

He took the bag from her and peered inside as she worked the key in the lock. "Ah. I see that. So I wanted to ask you your professional opinion on the creature."

The creature. That's how he referred to adorable Polpetto. He played the reluctant pet owner, but he was fooling no one. Polpetto accompanied him everywhere, and sometimes she'd catch him smiling like a kid on Christmas morning with pride over something his doggie had done. "What's that?"

"Digging. My garden's like a minefield. I have no idea what he's going after, but he's like a budding archaeologist. Is that normal?"

She shrugged as she opened the door, then sneezed at the volume of construction dust in the place. A home was supposed to be welcoming, warm … comforting. Yet, every time she walked through this door, all she did was sneeze and wish a fairy could wave its magic wand and make it livable. Not that she didn't like remodeling. In fact, she loved the idea … she just didn't have the hours in the day. "Yeah, it is. He probably needs more exercise, so just take him for an extra walk and you'll be fine," she said to him as he passed through. "Welcome to the funhouse."

"Oh, it's not so bad," he said to her, looking around.

Easy for him to say now. His house was nearly done. Just needed a few finishing touches. And actually, over the past few months, she'd managed to start tackling a couple rooms, so that when one entered the front door, they saw a sunny kitchen, a nice, sweeping staircase, and a modern bathroom, off to the side.

But venture a little farther than that, and … that's where the shiny façade crumbled away. The living room hadn't been touched, her garden out back was like a jungle, and the whole second floor probably needed to be condemned.

"I don't know how you can say that with a straight face," she said as she took the tomatoes from him and began to line them on the kitchen windowsill.

He shrugged. "So, what do you have in store for me tonight, boss?"

Luckily, her best friend since arriving in Mussomeli was a contractor, and a pretty darn good one. He was American, too, so they had a lot in common, and no language barrier, aside from some of his funny Southern sayings. When one ignored his off-color remarks and his double entendres, as well as his overinflated ego, he actually was a pretty great guy. Though she hadn't done much to her house, the things she had gotten done were mostly because of his help. He had been coming over every night that week to fix her mistakes, or lend a little bit of needed height or elbow grease to her operations.

But she hadn't really wanted him here today. She was *sure* she'd told him she had someplace else to be.

"Well, I think if you can just help me install these shelves, I can mark the kitchen as done," she said, pointing to some floating shelves she wanted to put over the bistro table. "Then I only have five million other things on my to-do-list."

"No problem," he said, reaching into his tool belt. "I'll get that done in a jiffy. How are you at getting things under code?"

"Code?" It was a deer-in-the-headlights moment. She knew that code was important, but she'd been ignoring it as much as possible. "Well, I haven't really looked into that lately. Probably not very good."

"You might want to look into it. The new inspector in town is a real hard nut to crack. He's giving everyone the runaround."

"He is?"

"Yeah. He came over yesterday. Gave me a whole bunch of crap about my new porch railing not being regulation."

Great. They'd recently had to deal with a tough-as-nails councilwoman before, who'd made life for all ex-pats difficult, until her untimely demise. The town of Mussomeli, as much as it wanted to fill these empty buildings and revitalize itself, hadn't been all that easy to get along with.

"What's wrong with your porch railing?"

"It extended an inch too far into the street, or something. Not even an inch. Like, a *millimeter* too far." He held up his fingers to demonstrate.

Audrey winced. If they were that strict, they'd likely find a million things wrong with Audrey's place.

Mason turned to the wall, and on cue, Audrey's stomach rumbled. She hadn't had anything to eat since a banana at breakfast.

"Well … in the meantime … did you eat dinner?" she asked, peering in the empty refrigerator, hoping he'd say he had.

"No. Is that an invitation, Boston?" He stood there with his drill, smirking.

"Actually, it's a cry for help. I don't exactly have…" She opened up her pantry to show him how pathetic it was. It was actually even worse than she remembered. All she saw was a half-package of spaghetti and a jar of pimento olives she'd meant to use for a recipe, but never got around to it.

7

He tilted his head. "What are you talking about? You have plenty of stuff."

She squinted into the cabinet. Of course, Mason wasn't a world-class chef or anything, but he could look at a collection of the most unappetizing ingredients on earth and come up with something delicious. Everything he touched turned to gold, which was sometimes hard to stomach, because unfortunately, he knew it. If he'd been a girl, Audrey would've been insanely jealous. "Um. For what?"

He plugged in the bit on the drill and gave it a couple of good whirrs. "You've got tomatoes. You've got pasta. Make spaghetti. You can handle that?"

She frowned, hating to admit that most of her pasta prior to coming to Sicily was consumed with a nice helping of jarred Prego atop it. She'd never even made pasta from *cans* of crushed tomatoes. And using fresh tomatoes seemed like a massive undertaking for someone who'd just been working ten hours at her job. Plus, she did have that important date to get ready for in … she checked her phone. An hour.

She yawned at the thought of it and rummaged through a drawer for a take-out menu. "How about if I order us some *maccu di fave* from the Mercado del Pepe? It's delish."

The Mercado del Pepe was the nearest supermarket. Audrey was probably their best customer of late, not for groceries, but for their *maccu di fave* and fresh bread.

He shrugged. "No clue what that is."

"It's soup! With fava beans. It's so good."

He made a face. "Beans? Pass."

"Have you ever eaten a vegetable in your life?"

"Beans aren't vegetables."

"Uh. Yes, they are."

"Whatever. I'm surprised you don't want to go to that café of yours."

Mason meant La Mela Verde. That was the nearest café, where she'd been eating most of her meals ever since she arrived in town. But she knew for a fact that Mason steered clear of it, not because he didn't like the food, but because of the owner, G. Audrey and G had been sharing a bit of a flirtation, and though Mason would never say as much, Audrey got the feeling he was a little jealous.

She hated to admit that the reason she *didn't* want to go there now was because she'd accepted an invitation from G for eight that night, to come over and sample his new dessert menu.

G had called it a date. But it wasn't, really. At least, she didn't think so. G was a friendly guy who had a long list of social engagements. She was just doing him a favor, like Mason was doing for her.

Or maybe …

"Well, I—" She checked the time on her phone again. Fifty-eight minutes to go.

When she looked up, he was holding the shelf up to the wall, but staring at her curiously. "You got somewhere to be, Boston?"

"Um … well, yes. I did promise G I'd taste-test some of his new desserts."

"Ah." He turned to the wall so that she couldn't see his face and started drilling. Did he do that deliberately?

"You know me, I never could say no to free tiramisu!" she said lightly, opening the Mercado del Pepe takeout menu.

He didn't respond. Instead, she watched him install the shelving effortlessly, not taking a break, almost as if *he* was the one who was in a rush. When he was done, he shoved his tools in his toolbox and patted his side for Polpetto. "You know what? Forget the soup. I'm not really hungry, and I can tell your mind is somewhere else," he said, heading for the door. "Besides, my momma's at my place. She probably made something for me."

Right. His mother had been visiting for the past few weeks, from Charleston. "But—"

"See you tomorrow," he said, slipping out the door before she even had a chance to pet Polpetto goodbye.

She sighed, feeling cold, wondering if she should apologize. But she didn't have time to worry about it. Maybe it was better that he left, anyway. She had to get ready for her date. Non-date. Whatever.

She rushed up the stairs, wondering what she should wear, a flutter of excitement in her chest.

CHAPTER TWO

As Audrey walked toward La Mela Verde, she quickly jabbed in a text to Brina, who with the time difference, was probably making breakfast. *Going to see G now. Nervous.*

Her older sister, Brina, who was back home in Boston, had pretty much been married to her husband forever, and they had three adorable rugrats to show for it. Brina was the sister who always had a date on Saturday night.

Audrey was the one who usually stayed home on weekends, nose buried in a book.

No, her love life never had been much to write home about. In Boston, it'd been one long string of losers. Here in Sicily, things seemed to be turning around. She had Mason, who gave her heart a little flutter every time she looked at him.

And then there was G, the owner of the café, who was good-looking, charming, kind, and probably the best chef she'd ever met.

Definite possibilities.

But though she'd been bouncing around between the two of them, she'd be the first to admit she was too naïve with men to know for sure if either of them was worth writing home about. Mason was so beautiful as to be virtually unattainable, probably more of a Hollywood-level crush than anything else. And G was just so friendly to *everyone*, she wasn't sure if he was treating her specially because he liked her, or because he was just being G.

Even so, she'd built this up into a big turning point in their relationship. Before now, it'd just been hugs. Hearty cheek-kisses. He'd held her hand once. But here, with the two of them alone, was a chance for him to finally lay down his cards and show her his true intentions. And as exciting as it was, it also made her nervous. There was a little voice in the back of her head that said, *So how are you going to screw this up now?*

A second later, Brina's response came back: *Go get him! Remember, you are a beautiful, confident woman, and he is lucky to be with you.*

10

She sucked in a breath and let it out, feeling absolutely none of that confidence. *I'll try.*

Good luck. I want details later.

She shivered, but was forced out of the thought when she rounded a bend and found G outside, in his typical white apron and skull cap. No, he hadn't dressed for the occasion, but what did she expect? He'd been working all day. It didn't make him look any less handsome. He looked so cool there, smoking a cigarette, with his shirt sleeves rolled up to expose his tattooed, well-formed biceps. He snuffed it out as she arrived and gave a big, friendly wave.

"Ah, *Principessa*! I was missing you!" he said, rushing to meet her. He grasped her shoulders firmly and gave a double-cheek kiss, gazing down at her adoringly. "You are so beautiful in that little dress. My heart is melting right out of my chest, into a puddle."

Now she was glad she'd worn her sexy, pink, off-the-shoulder number. At first, she'd thought it showed too much skin, or was too youthful for a woman of thirty-two, but G's gaze of appreciation told her otherwise.

Of course, this is big. Of course, this is special, she thought as he took her hand and gently kissed her knuckles. Then he guided her inside the candlelit room.

She walked into the darkened café, a little shocked by how large it looked when it was empty. Usually, it was packed with people coming from all over Mussomeli to enjoy G's specialties. The man was kind of a fixture in Mussomeli, known by just about everyone in town. Now, she could really see the décor, the beige stucco walls, the casks of wine lining the small dining area, the small bistro tables lined up along one end of the room, with the tiny tile bar in the corner.

"Oh, there's no one else here?" she asked, feigning surprise, though he'd told her before it would be just the two of them.

"Of course! I want your opinion, my dear, and I need you to have no distractions. After all, who better to taste test the sweets than the sweet?" he said with a charming wink.

She went up to the counter and found that he'd already placed the food in a line in front of her, ready to be sampled. The presentation was absolutely gorgeous—these were no everyday cannoli and tiramisu. They looked like works of art, every one of them, on dainty doilies, drizzled with powdered sugar and dark chocolate ganache. The man knew how to make masterpieces from his food. Her mouth instantly began to water.

"Gorgeous. But you will need a truck to move me if I eat all of these."

He chuckled and went back behind the counter as she pulled herself onto a stool. He poured her a cup of tea with lemon, and she smiled at his knowing her favorite drink. "Who knows? They may be absolutely terrible."

Now it was her turn to laugh. Never had G made anything to eat that was short of incredible. He was a true artist when it came to this stuff. Sometimes she'd imagine being his wife, and him bringing her breakfast in bed every morning. She'd definitely start to tip the scales, probably before she put on her wedding dress.

"I doubt that. They look amazing." She picked up a fork. "Which one should I try first?"

He reached over, cut off a piece of a thick, chocolate-covered cookie with pistachios on top, and slid it onto a plate. He said, "This one. *Rame di Napoli*."

She eagerly took a bite of it. The chocolate combined with hints of honey, orange, and cinnamon in an altogether delicious taste sensation. She instinctively let out an *Mmmmm*. "Anyone ever tell you that you are an absolute Picasso of the kitchen?"

He smiled and went down the line, cutting off a piece of a little green marzipan cake with a cherry on top and passing it over to her. "*Cassata*," he said, though she was still eyeing the cookies, wanting to finish them off. That banana she'd put in her stomach for breakfast clearly wasn't doing it.

She tasted, getting flavors of ricotta and liquor, possibly brandy. It wasn't her favorite, but it was still delicious. "Wow."

"You approve?"

"Yes, I do. These two should definitely be on your menu."

"All right. You said it, it will be done!" he said, gesticulating in his wild, larger-than-life way that made her giggle.

He moved to the next, which was the miniature cannoli. She'd never liked cannoli, but she sampled that, too, and as expected, it did not disappoint. She nodded, mouth full, as he waited for her verdict. She gave a thumbs-up. "Delicious."

He laughed. "You look so gorgeous, *Principessa*, with your mouth full of my food!" he said, leaning closer. He had a napkin in his hand, which he used to gently wipe the powdered sugar from her lips.

Her breath hitched as he stared into her eyes. Was this really ... was he finally going to... .?

Suddenly, the bell over the door jingled, and they broke apart like two magnets of the opposite charge. Before Audrey could crane her neck to peer around the dessert case, G erupted with, "Luigi! *Buonasera!*"

Those were the only two words Audrey understood as G launched into a long Italian monologue to his new arrivals. It was an older couple, consisting of a rather thick, goateed man in a polo shirt that hugged his body in a way that reminded Audrey of a sausage leaking from its casing, and an older woman in a black dress dotted with daisies and Keds-like sneakers. Audrey couldn't be sure, but she thought she'd seen that couple somewhere before, somewhere in Mussomeli …

She hoped he'd wave them goodbye and send them on their way. But whatever G was saying, it didn't seem like he wanted them to leave anytime soon. Indeed, when they came in and looked like they were about to sit down on the stools on either side of Audrey, she quickly got up and moved so they could sit together. They settled in, as if they were prepared to stay there for the duration.

G finished whatever he was saying to them and smiled at Audrey. "*Principessa.* Do you know Carmen and Luigi Marino? They are from il Mercado del Pepe, the little place down the street?"

"Oh! That's where I recognize you two from," Audrey said, shaking their hands. "I love your *maccu di fave.*"

The woman stared at her blankly, until G translated. Her eyes widened.

"*Ah. Grazie!*" the woman said, smiling.

"Hey. Are you cheating on me?" G said, giving Audrey a sly wink. He nodded at the couple. "They don't speak English so very well. But I must tell you, they are the best of cooks themselves, so I thought, who better to sample my food, eh? I'm glad they took me up on the invitation."

"Right," Audrey murmured, confused. He'd invited them? What happened to: *Who better to taste test the sweets than the sweet?* She sighed as he gave them some of the cookie she'd wanted more of. *He was just buttering you up, silly. Using his Sicilian charm.*

He'd been so close to … to … well, she wasn't sure what he would've done. A romantic kiss? Maybe it finally would've moved them beyond flirting into something … real. That was all she wanted.

Her spirits nose-dived and her shoulders slumped. She crossed her arms over her dress as they conversed animatedly in Italian. Now, she just felt foolish. Overdressed. When he'd invited her, she'd texted

Brina, telling her how nervous and excited she was to have some real alone-time with him. Apparently, G hadn't been thinking of alone-time with her, at all. And now, she dreaded her next text to Brina. Just another let-down in a long line of disappointments.

Instinctively, she yawned, picked up her purse, and slipped off her stool.

G finally took that moment to turn to her. "Where are you going? You have not yet tried my *granita. Pistachio, mandorla e cioccolato*? Come. You pick.*"

She shook her head. "Sounds great, but I'm actually really tired. And I have a big day at work tomorrow. Lots of appointments. So I'll take a raincheck. I'm sorry! But thank you so much! It was really great!"

He shrugged without the slightest hint of disappointment, though he did come around the counter to escort her to the door as she said goodbye to the other couple. He walked her outside and once again put his hands on her shoulders. This time, he gave her a kiss on the forehead. "*Sogni d'oro. Dormi bene*," he said. Sweet dreams. Sleep well.

"Thank you. And thank you for inviting me over to sample your menu. I am sure you'll have a hit on your hands, as usual," she said, as she turned to walk away.

Part of her hoped he'd call her back, give her that kiss that would knock her socks off, but he didn't. It was a sad-trumpets ending, for sure.

On the way home, she tried to keep her spirits light. Nick walked by her side, faithful and as cute as could be. It was a beautiful night, and the sun was just setting, painting orange and pink streaks through the sky, just beyond the old buildings and olive trees on the western edge of town. In the distance, Mussomeli Castle rose up on the neighboring mountainside, a single, stalwart guardian of the walled city. The sky beyond it was breathtaking and bracing.

But she couldn't help feeling, after everything with G, a little sad. Truthfully, she wasn't really sure she liked him in that way at all. Maybe she was just feeling the ticking of her biological clock and latching onto the closest thing that made sense. She wanted everything Brina had, and part of her had wanted to escape Boston because it seemed like a dead end when it came to men. But maybe everywhere in the world would be the same. Maybe it was just her destiny to be alone forever.

Before she got home, she realized she already had another text from Brina. One word: *Details.*

Not wanting to go into it anymore, she typed in one word of her own: *Fizzled.*

At that, a tear threatened to make its way out of her eye. She quickly swiped it away before she could turn this into a full-on pity party.

Her sister replied with probably the only thing that would've made her feel better at that moment: *Sorry honey. Oh, well. His loss. So ... what about Abs?*

"Abs" was Mason. Yes, he did have a nice set of those, which he liked to show off whenever possible. But right now, she'd had her fill of men, and just wanted to settle down with a nice big bowl of ...

Nothing. She forgot. There was nothing in her kitchen to eat.

Probably better that way. A pint of gelato would probably not make it thirty seconds in my possession.

When she got inside her cold home, Nick was dutifully waiting for her in the foyer. She reached down and petted him, then looked around. Mason had done a good job with the shelving, but it was like putting a Band-Aid on a gunshot wound. She had the railing on the stairs to fix. Then there was plastering the wall in the living area. And then refinishing the hardwood floors. And of course, the wallpaper would have to come down—

She sighed. The more she thought about that growing laundry list, the sicker she felt.

"Besides," she said aloud to herself, "one thing at a time is all we can do."

Audrey blinked. Where had that come from? That was one of her dad's famous sayings. He was a contractor, too, before he walked out on his family when she was barely twelve years old. At that time, she'd been her father's right hand as he fixed up all those old mansions on the Back Bay. He was always patient, always level-headed, even when the house was a complete ruin that seemed impossible to rehabilitate. Whenever they'd first arrive at a mansion, he'd stroke the graying stubble on his chin, grab his hammer, and say, "One thing at a time is all we can do."

For some reason, that made her feel better, as she climbed the stairs to her room and got into her pajamas. Even though he'd left her without any explanation, she'd always been his mini-me. Every time she had a problem, he'd come to her bedside and tuck her in and talk to her about it.

And then, one day … poof. He was gone.

It was hazy now, exactly what had happened. Her mother was so bitter, she never liked to speak of it. Brina was bitter, too … but she hadn't been dad's favorite. Audrey had found herself with no one to talk to about it, and an ever-widening hole of wonder inside her. Where was he now? What was he up to? And most importantly, why hadn't he tried to get in touch, not once, in twenty years?

When she snuggled into bed, Nick jumped in with her, and she was glad of that. She needed something so she didn't feel so alone. She cuddled close to him, savoring his warm fur.

But she was so tired, she fell asleep almost the second her head hit the pillow. And again, as she'd done many times before, she had a vision of her dad. He looked the same as he had twenty years ago, with his cropped blond hair and tanned skin, strong and more like a California surfer type than a buttoned-up East Coast city dweller. Her dream was the same as always—Audrey, following him through a massive house under construction, the intoxicating smell of sawdust and fresh paint in her nostrils, his voice echoing and far away as he pointed out things that needed to be done.

At least, it always *started* the same. It ended differently sometimes, usually with his voice fading away and then when she'd follow him into a room, he'd be gone. She'd wind up chasing after him, calling for him and rushing from room to room as if in a labyrinth or funhouse maze, trying to find him, but getting hopelessly lost and confused.

No matter what, though, what started happily always seem to dissolve to a kind of hysteria, because the little girl in the dream knew that eventually, he'd be gone, and she could do nothing to stop him. Sometimes she'd try to grab his hand, but he'd always pull away.

This time, as she followed him, she tried again. Just as she slipped her hand in his, he pulled away. "Dad!" she cried, her heart in her throat, knowing he was about to disappear. "Please." He stopped for a moment and looked back at her, before shoving a hand into the pocket of his flannel shirt to grab his cigarettes. As he did, a folded piece of cardstock fluttered out and landed on the ground.

She reached forward, picked it up, and realized it was a postcard of a beautiful place, with a warm sunset and mirror-like dark water. In the back, melting into the pink-clouded skies, a black mountain range. Two seagulls soared peaceful arcs in the air. The card itself was dog-eared and well-loved.

She stared at the postcard wistfully, as her father took it from her hands. "You like that? Someday, we'll go there. It's called—"

Suddenly, Nick made a screeching noise and she woke with a start, sitting up bolt upright in bed. She looked around to find him scampering into the corner, pin eyes glowing in the minimal light cast through the shutters by the moon.

She groaned. He'd probably found yet another mouse. She flipped on the light. Sure enough, he was terrorizing a poor little gray thing, making it shake in its boots. "Hey, tough guy," she said, grabbing a tissue box from the night table and removing the few remaining tissues. "Pick on someone your own size. Back off."

She snapped her fingers and when he resisted, she nudged him away and knelt down, trying to get the mouse into the tissue box. Unfortunately, the thing was too scared. As she tried to guide it into her little trap, she thought about her dream. That thing with the postcard had actually happened, hadn't it?

Yes, it had. He'd kept a postcard in the breast pocket of his flannel shirt. When she asked him about it, he'd gotten a little wistful. And yes, he'd told her he would take her there someday. It was a real place, on this earth, a place he'd desperately wanted to go to, since why hold something close to your heart, day in and day out, unless it meant a lot to you?

He'd called the place …

She strained to think of it, but it didn't come to her. She couldn't remember.

She was so busy trying to fish an answer out of her sleep-addled mind that the mouse quickly scampered away through a hole underneath the picture window. She sighed and stood up. Nick was already back on her bed, lounging like King Tut in the exact center of it, making it difficult to squeeze in. "Thanks, buddy. You woke me up so you could get most of the bed, huh?"

When he didn't move, she nudged him, but that didn't do any good. Either he was already asleep, or he was pretending to be.

Positioning herself in the very side of the bed, she pulled up the covers and tucked herself in, thinking of the postcard. Where was that place? Had her father gone there when he ran away? It only made sense. But water, mountains, beautiful sunsets … it could be absolutely anywhere.

And some small part of her hated those beautiful vistas, if they were the thing that finally pulled her dad away from her.

As she drifted off to sleep, she decided it really wasn't much of a clue at all, and the only way she'd ever find her father now was if he found her.

CHAPTER THREE

The following day, as Audrey stepped out the door to head to work, she saw her neighbor across the street, Nessa.

Nessa was a blonde bombshell from California and supposedly soon-to-be star of her own HGTV reality television show, which she never stopped talking about. But worse than that, despite Audrey's friendly overtures, Nessa had always been icy to her. She'd even accused her of murder. Twice.

Needless to say, their relationship had always been a little rocky.

So Audrey cringed when she saw her outside, talking to a bald man with a clipboard. As she continued up the road toward the clinic, she tried to ignore the conversation, which was easy, since both of them were speaking Italian, a language she still wasn't very good at, despite all her best efforts.

"Hey, Audrey?" a voice called behind her, before she could make a clean getaway.

Audrey turned, surprised by the tone of voice. Nessa usually spoke to her in a way that was either dismissive or downright annoyed. "Yeah?"

The man in the clipboard was getting into his little car. Nessa, looking as gorgeous as if a makeup crew had worked on her for hours, sauntered over to her, holding the white puffball of a kitten she'd adopted last week. "Weren't you going to say hi to me, neighbor?"

Audrey raised an eyebrow as she gave the kitten a visual examination to make sure its owner was treating it well. "You seemed busy. Not to mention that you usually tear into me whenever I do."

"Oh, no I don't. At least, not today," she said, flipping her long ponytail over her shoulder. "I'm in such a good mood, I could probably do a cartwheel, right here! The inspector just came and gave me his seal of approval. So now I can give the studio a green light to start filming!"

"I thought you already had the seal of approval. You've been doing so much renovation already," she said, confused.

She scoffed. "Are you kidding? Those renovations were just to make this place livable, so I wouldn't be existing in a glorified pigpen.

19

I told the studio that they needed to keep their talent happy, and as long as I was living there, I expected certain things, otherwise they'd need to book me a place at the hotel. Of course, they agreed. Anyway, *now* the real work can begin."

"Real work?" Audrey stared at the house across from her, a sick feeling blooming in her gut. The place was gorgeous. They'd painted the outside of the house a gorgeous burnt sienna, and the windows and Baroque-style fixtures and balcony scrollwork were the stuff of Mediterranean dreams. Though Audrey had only been inside once, what she had seen had been equally impressive—like something from an interior design brochure, or Martha Stewart's living room.

"Of course. But I was worried. That inspector is tough. He came by a few days ago with a laundry list of complaints."

"A laundry list?" Now, Audrey felt even sicker. This had to be the guy Mason was talking about. But if he'd had complaints about Nessa's Palace of Perfection, he'd likely put a big CONDEMNED sign on the front door of Audrey's.

She nodded. "But it's all taken care of. Whew, that's a load off."

"Wow. The inspector hasn't even *contacted* me yet. Is that normal?"

"He will. It's kind of like a death and taxes thing. The inspector was telling me that he's pretty behind, so he probably won't get to your house for a while. So consider this a warning and get yourself ready!"

"Oh." While that was good news, Audrey had the distinct feeling that given an entire *year* to get the place up to code, she'd still be working up to the wire. "What happens if he finds fault with the place?"

"He gives you a citation and a certain amount of time to fix it."

"And if you don't?" *Or more likely, can't?*

"I don't know. Probably condemns the place and shoves you out and tells you not to let the door hit you in the butt." She peered behind Audrey's shoulder at her home, and Audrey bristled, knowing what was coming. "How are things going with yours?"

"Um … okay," she lied. "Obviously, it's hard, with the clin—"

"You should be fine. He was also telling me about some real horror stories. In one house, they hadn't even switched out the plumbing or wiring! Can you imagine?"

Audrey nearly choked. She hadn't done that. Hadn't even thought of that. Well she had, but the plumbing was copper and looked to be in good shape, and Mason had said the electricity wasn't terrible.

20

She clutched her belly, the sick feeling becoming a full-on stomachache.

"Anyway, I wanted to ask you about my little Snowball," she said, holding up the kitten.

She stared at the animal. He'd once been known as Lambchop, which was adorable. "Snowball? You renamed him?"

She nodded. "Of course. Couldn't have her with that terrible name."

Of course she'd name her Snowball, probably the most unimaginative name for a white animal on earth. "Everything all right?"

Nessa frowned. "Well ... I don't know. She had some crud in her eye this morning. It was so gross! Is that anything I should be worried about?"

Audrey peered closer at the tiny kitten. "It could be worrisome, but it looks clear now. It might be from the construction dust, and the fact that it's a new environment. If it continues, I can prescribe some drops." She checked her phone. "With that being said, I've got to get over to the clinic. I have a nine o'clock appointment."

She turned and headed down the street, now more worried than ever about the renovations. She did have the weekend to work on it. Maybe she could beg Mason to come over and help her. But ... was Mason angry at her? She hadn't really thought about it much since she had her "date" with G to plan for, but they had left things awkwardly.

Maybe she'd be stuck handling all the renovations herself.

Wishing she could be rich or funded by a television studio and hire people to help with her project like Nessa had, she arrived at the clinic to find a cardboard box waiting for her. Great. She let out a heavy breath, knowing exactly what that meant. Sure enough, when she peered inside, she found a litter of squirmy little bunnies, only a couple days old. Four of them, to be exact.

Wonderful. Wild bunnies. It was likely whoever brought them there thought they were doing good, but the truth was, bunny moms only come back to the nest at night, to feed their young. Likely, this do-gooder mistakenly thought they'd been abandoned. Now, without a mother to care for them, they had little chance of survival. To give them the best chance possible, they'd need good care, an incubator to keep their temperatures up. She brought them into the back room and set the box down, feeling their little bodies. They were still warm, but they needed immediate help.

21

Just then, though, someone rang the bell at reception. She rushed to the front, expecting to see her nine o'clock, which according to the appointment log, was a German Shepherd. The man there was well-dressed, in a tailored suit with a red tie, and a lot of long, slicked-back hair. He reminded Audrey of a stockbroker as he stood there, eyes volleying around the room as if scanning the Wall Street ticker.

"Hello!" Audrey went to the desk, craning her neck to see around it, but no. No dog. If it was a German Shepherd, it was either very small, or invisible. "You forget something?" she asked with a smile.

"Actually, no. I'm looking for a Dr. Smart?" the man said in almost perfectly unaccented English.

"That's me."

"American? I'm American, too. Born and raised in Tulsa. You?"

"Boston."

"Fantastic!" He whipped a business card from his pocket and held it out to her as if presenting her with some wondrous gift.

She read the words on the front—*Eton Scarletto, Commercial Developer*—and almost laughed. Certainly he'd come into the wrong place, if he wanted anything to do with her little clinic. Other than being in a good area of town, her clinic was very bare-bones, the result of having to transform it from a broken-down old vacuum store to a working vet center in less than a week. "What can I help you with, Mr. Scarletto?"

"I'm a recent expat like you, and a leading developer here in Mussomeli, and one of the things I've been tasked with by the city is bringing more business to the area to meet the demand of the influx of people like you and me, with more sophisticated consumer needs. I think I have a great opportunity you might be interested in," he said, continuing to scan the place, sizing it up. For what, she still didn't know.

"Me? Are you sure?"

"Yes. Of course," he said, leaning forward. His slicked-back hair was so shiny that the fluorescent light above reflected on it. "You've heard of PetSense?"

Of course she'd heard of it. It was only one of the biggest pet superstores in America. There was a PetSense on nearly every corner in Boston. They'd pretty much decimated all other competition. The jingle instantly came to her head, since she'd heard it about a million times in her lifetime. "You mean ..." and she sang, "'PetSense Makes Sense!' That PetSense?"

He laughed at her singing, and rightly so, since she couldn't carry a tune to save her life. "That's right. They're the best."

"Yes. But what does that—"

"They are one of my clients. Great people, too. And what I'm envisioning is a little partnership," he said with a wide smile with perfectly straight white teeth. "You wouldn't even have to move. The storefront next door is up for lease. Think about it. There's lots you can do with this space. We can make your clinic part of our in-store services, including our pet boutique, pet supplies, pet grooming services … we'll be a one-stop shop for all things pets."

Yes, they would be. She had no doubt that they'd add the same slickness to her operation that they'd done to all the little mom-and-pop shops she remembered growing up in Boston. But they were so … corporate. Smarmy, almost. She was sure there'd been some bad press about them getting their animals from puppy mills and mistreating them. Plus, *corporate* had never been her thing. Audrey had always preferred patronizing smaller establishments for everything from hair products to tuna fish. And that was one of the things she *loved* about Mussomeli: No Walmart-like stores.

She started to shake her head and hand the card back to him. "Thanks, but—"

He held up a hand suddenly, silencing her. "I think you'll be surprised by what you can do here. What's your profit margin like?"

"Uh. I haven't really thought about that … I don't know." *How about, zero?* "But I only just started. I'm just settling in and really can't even think about expand—"

"Come on. Stop thinking small potatoes. If you want to grow, you've got to—"

"Like I said, at this point, it's just about getting settled, so I don't think I can grow," she said to him, finally succeeding in planting the card back into his palm. She didn't have time for this. Those bunnies in the back room needed her. "I'm happy being independent and I'm really not interested in adding all those services. But I appreciate you coming by."

He shrugged and made a point of placing the card on the counter. He tapped on it twice. "All right. But if you change your mind, there's my number. Give me a call."

He mimed holding a phone receiver to his cheek with his thumb and pinky, and winked in a *let's-do-lunch* kind of way.

"Thanks," she said, waiting until he'd closed the door to toss the business card in the trash and murmuring under her breath, "Just like a used car salesman. Probably trying to sell me a lemon."

Then, thinking better of it, she grabbed the business card from the empty trash can and tucked it in her purse. He'd paid for those business cards, after all. It seemed like a waste of a perfectly good tree to just toss it. If anything, she could use it as scrap paper. She never had a spare piece of scrap paper when she needed it.

She looked at her schedule and realized she had a block of open time. Perfect. Those bunnies were calling for their care. Time to get some things done.

*

After getting the bunnies—Peter, Flopsy, Mopsy, and Cottontail, which wasn't much more original than Nessa had been, but hey, she was too busy to be creative!— set up in a nice warm nest with a heat lamp, Audrey checked her schedule and realized she didn't have another appointment until two. So she decided to take the time to rush back to the house and make a list of things that needed to be done right away, just in case the inspector should come by. On the way, she picked up some *maccu di fave* from Pepe.

Already tired and still a little defeated after her conversation with Nessa, she sat down at her kitchen table with Nick at her heels and began making that list. On top of the paper, she placed the big things. The roof, for instance, which she'd patched a little, really needed to be entirely replaced, and she'd have to price the slate at the hardware store. The toilet in the upstairs bathroom had never worked right. And there was still a massive hole in the floorboards between the first and second floor. She'd placed a plank of wood over it so she wouldn't unwittingly fall through, but that was a stopgap measure. She kept tripping over the uneven place where the plank met the actual floor. The whole floor and subflooring probably needed to be replaced.

By the time she'd scooped the first spoonful of soup into her mouth, the list was already two pages long.

Thank goodness for the soup. It instantly made her feel better. Calmer. She took a few more hearty spoonfuls, savoring the garlicky taste of the broth. *Okay, yes, things are not going so well with the renovation. But all in good time. It will get done. Remember what Dad said? One thing at a time is all we can do.*

24

She clasped and unclasped her hand to get rid of the cramp from writing so much, and smiled, her strength renewed. As she was about to start again on the list of smaller, more cosmetic things she'd have to look into, someone knocked on the door. Immediately, Nick hissed.

"Oh, calm down, little fighter. Since when have we ever had anyone show up at this door who warrants that kind of response?" she said to him, wondering who could be knocking in the middle of the day. Pretty much everyone she knew, knew that she worked all day at the clinic. *Well, maybe Nessa. Sometimes even I feel like hissing at her.*

She went to the door and opened it to a short, bald man with a mustache.

She was about to tell him he had the wrong door when she noticed the clipboard in his hand. In Boston, kids were always around her apartment building with clipboards, selling magazine subscriptions. Did they have that in Sicily?

But …she'd seen him before, somewhere … oh, right.

With Nessa.

Her heart shuddered to a stop inside her chest.

Oh, no, she thought. *He isn't … he can't be …*

The man frowned down at the clipboard and said, "Miss Smart? I am Vito Cascarelli. I am the city building inspector." He reached into his pocket, pulled out some credentials, and flashed them to her. "May I come in?"

Oh god. He is.

Audrey's stomach dropped, and she grabbed hold of the door jamb for support. She no longer had an appetite. Not even for that delicious *maccu di fave.*

CHAPTER FOUR

Audrey stared at the man, wide-eyed, for at least ten seconds, before she realized this was her cue to say something, and it would probably not be polite to sit there, gaping at him for the rest of the day.

It didn't matter. The man was clearly intent on coming in, regardless of what she did. He took a step closer, and she moved away just as he walked through, scanning the place like it was a new planet he'd just landed on.

"Hello," she said, several beats too late. "Of course, Mr. Cascarelli. How are you? Can I get you a cup of tea?"

He shook his head brusquely. "That will be unnecessary. This is a quick visit. I'd just like to take a look around, if you have a few minutes?"

"Uh … sure …" she said, now scanning the place as critically as he was. She realized that she'd probably left her underwear on the bedroom floor this morning in her haste to get ready, but now that was the least of her problems. "I didn't expect you. I really wasn't able to do very much, considering it's so short notice—"

"Fine, fine. Just … lead the—" He stopped short when he caught sight of Nick, sitting on the Travertine tile in the kitchen, but did not comment. Besides, she had a license to keep him, so it was cool, right? She hoped. The way he was looking around, eyes slitted critically, she felt as if she was violating laws, just by existing. "Uh, lead the way. Please."

"Oh. Okay. You should probably know," she tittered, "that I'm actually a vet in the center of town. So I've been spending a lot of time doing two renovations, which means I really haven't had as much time as I'd like to—"

"You're Dottore Smart?" he asked, flipping pages on his clipboard.

She nodded.

He pulled a pencil from behind his ear and tapped the page. "I have the vet center on my list, too. I'll get there. It's a long list, as you can imagine, so I'd like to get this underway as quickly as possible."

Audrey groaned inwardly. Great. "Well, I guess we should get started," she said, planting her feet in the kitchen. "Here, you see, is the kitchen."

He walked around, scratching the side of his temple with the eraser end of his pencil. Flipped on the lights. Ran the water. Got down on his knees and checked under the cabinets. Made a few noncommittal *mmmhmm* noises that could've been either bad or good.

Then he turned to her, expectant.

She led him to the small bathroom off the kitchen. She'd renovated that, too, mostly with Mason's help, and while at first she'd thought the shower was possessed, lately, it'd been very well-behaved. From the door, she heard him reach into the shower and turn on the faucet. She gave herself a mental fist-bump when it didn't moan in protest as it started up.

He ducked out of the shower and nodded at her. "Great light fixture."

Wait, was that a compliment? That was actually ... not the *This place is unfit for swine!* comment she'd been expecting. "Thanks ..." she said carefully, half-expecting a "but" to come on the end of it, like *Great light fixture, but it's actually not up to code.*

Surprisingly, it didn't come. Pride swelled in her chest. *He likes my taste in lighting! We're on the same level. Practically best friends!*

She wished desperately that he would say, "I've seen enough! This place is glorious!" and give her a bright, golden stamp on her record that she could show happily to Nessa and everyone else. That didn't happen, though.

When it didn't, she hoped that something—a phone call, a swarm of killer bees—would come in, pulling him away from his set course before he had a chance to get to the worst areas of the house.

That did not happen either, unfortunately. Instead, he said, "Next?"

So reluctantly she led him up the short set of stairs to the first landing, which included the giant living room. It was a beautiful room, a room that made people see possibilities, but unfortunately, her renovations hadn't touched it. The wallpaper was peeling, there were giant pits in the floor right down to the dirt subflooring, and the old furniture inside was moth-eaten and dusty.

She was pretty sure he cringed when he looked around it. He flipped the lights, which worked, scribbled something on his clipboard, and motioned for her to continue the tour.

She brought him upstairs, and as she did, she felt the need to explain. "Yeah, well, you'll see that I really haven't touched the second floor. I haven't been able to get as much as I—"

"Well, you're a busy woman. All those pets need you."

Audrey turned back and was surprised to find him smiling kindly at her.

"Um, yes … right. Thanks."

She turned the corner and opened the door to the bathroom for him. When he went to flush the toilet, Audrey broke out in a cold sweat, a drop of which trickled down her rib cage. She hugged herself as it made a sick, loud choking noise that sounded like an animal drowning. "Sorry. That toilet gives me a little trouble."

He shrugged. "It makes the typical glug-glug-glugging sound it's supposed to when the bowl is emptied, which is fine," he said, scribbling more notes. "No problems."

"Really?" she said, shocked.

"Yes, that's right," he said as she stepped aside to let him into the guest bedroom. He looked around and nodded. "Looking good, looking good. I understand it's a work in progress, but you are making positive changes, so I'm definitely impressed with what you've done so far."

"That's right," she repeated, relief sweeping over her as she led him into the final room, her bedroom. "I'm so glad you—"

"What's that?"

She followed his outstretched finger to the floor. Sure enough, she'd left her red lace panties right there, near the foot of her bed.

She blushed and rushed ahead to scoop them up and throw them in her laundry basket. "Whoops. Forgot to—"

"No. Not that," he said, his bushy eyebrows coming together. "*That.*"

Audrey realized he'd been pointing about a foot to the right, where she'd placed the plank of wood so she wouldn't fall through the ceiling. She tittered again. "Oh. That. I sometimes forget that's there, I've grown so used to it. There's a pretty big hole in the ceiling. I almost fell right through it the first day I came here! But I put that plank over it until I have the time to—"

"*Mmmhmm,*" he said, scribbling something on his paper.

Before, she hadn't been able to tell, but this one? This one was *definitely* not a "good" *Mmmhmm.*

"The rest of the floor is really stable, though." She jumped up and down a little to prove it. "Obviously I plan to fix it once I have the money and the time. Is there a problem?"

He nodded, and when he looked up from the clipboard, his brow was tented in sympathy. "I'm sorry, but a hole like that, no matter how big, can affect the structural integrity of the entire floor. It needs to be rectified right away."

"Oh, well of course I will. But I think I'd need to do the whole floor. It's obviously a big job so it'll take the money and manpower —"

He wasn't listening. He scribbled some more, ripped off a small piece of paper from his clipboard rather harshly, and handed it to her. She stared at it, unable to make heads or tails of the Italian words, written in red, at the top of the page. She wasn't sure she *wanted* to. "What is this?"

"I'm sorry I have to do this to you. But I'm going to have to revoke your CO."

"My ... what?"

"Your Certificate of Occupancy," he said, his voice soft, full of regret. He sniffled a little.

"Oh." That didn't sound good. She stared at the paper as understanding slowly dawned on her. "Wait. Are you saying that I can't ... you mean that you're forcing me out? I can't even live here anymore?"

The next time he spoke, it was grainy, as if he had a frog in his throat. "Well, you can, once it's fixed, of course, and reinspect—"

"But that's going to take forever!" She started looking around for somewhere to sit, because she felt a little faint. Finally, she collapsed on her bed. "I don't even have the money to handle a repair that big right now. Not to mention, I can't do something that big myself. I'd need ..."

She stopped when she looked up and realized that the man's face was starting to crumple. He took a couple big gulps of air, and his face reddened. For a second, she thought he might cry.

"I can't tell you how sorry I am. It really breaks my heart to do it."

"Oh. Okay." She swallowed the protests, knowing they'd do no good. "Thanks, I guess?"

With that, he *did* start to cry. No, not just cry. Weep. He dropped his clipboard, buried his face in his hands, and let out a big, heart-wrenching sob that sounded almost like a cow in distress.

For a moment, Audrey just stared. Then she reached over to her night table, found her tissue box, and offered one to him. "Are you okay, Mr. Cascarelli?"

He accepted the tissue, dotted it at his eyes, and blew his nose into it in one big honk. "Yeah, it's just that … I really hate this job. It's not what I expected at all! I thought it would be good. Nice. Getting to see the inside of homes, meeting people. But they all hate me. You see, it's not easy. It's never easy going around and being the bad guy. But that's all I have to do, day in, day out." He hung his head and let out several more big sobs.

She stood up and patted his back. "But you're just following the city's ordinances. That's what you have to do. To keep people safe. You're a *good* guy, really."

He didn't answer her. He probably hadn't heard her, considering how loud he was weeping. The poor softy. How could Mason have said he was a hard-ass? He was just doing his job.

She rubbed his back soothingly. "And don't forget, you get to make people happy when they pass inspection. That's a good thing. Right?"

He nodded. "Yeah. I guess."

She folded the slip of paper and tucked it in her pocket, then helped him downstairs. "Don't you worry about me," she said to him as she guided him to the door. "I understand completely. I'll get it taken care of."

When he turned back to her, eyes glassy with tears, he said, "But you don't have anywhere to stay!"

Trying to nudge away that awful truth, she somehow managed a smile. "Thank you for coming by. Don't worry about me, Mr. Cascarelli. I'll survive."

She closed the door and leaned against it, facing Nick, and the accommodating smile disappeared from her face. *Somehow.*

Audrey went to the table and picked up her soup. It was cold now, and her appetite was definitely gone. As she closed up the container, she checked her phone. Great. She was late for her appointments.

She ran upstairs and grabbed her bag, throwing everything she could think of inside. She'd likely have to stay at the clinic now… somewhere. Then she ran down to the kitchen, grabbed her carton of soup, motioned to Nick, and the two of them rushed outside.

CHAPTER FIVE

"Thanks for coming in. And thank you for adopting. If there's anything I can do, please don't hesitate to ask!" she told a young mother and her daughter, who were holding a gray cat they'd named Sorellina. She waved excitedly at them. "*In bocca al lupo.* And *ciao!*"

The moment the door was closed, she sighed and scanned the area, wondering what she could repurpose to make a comfortable bed. When they'd begun the renovations of the place, Mason had asked her if she wanted to make one of the back rooms into a bedroom, so she could stay overnight if necessary, but she'd opted for more storage and space for the animals, instead, since her home was only a couple blocks away.

Now, she was really regretting that decision. And regretting ever thinking that working on the clinic was more important than making sure she had a place to live. Without a home base, she was pretty much screwed.

As she looked around, she rubbed her back, already anticipating how sore it was going to be tomorrow. Aside from putting a few uncomfortable plastic chairs together, she didn't have much of a choice when it came to her comfort. Sadly, she'd been in such a rush to get back to work for her two o'clock that she'd packed hastily. She'd forgotten a blanket. Her favorite pillow.

And—ugh—her toothbrush.

This was her late night at the clinic. It was after nine. As she went to the window to pull down the shade, she heard a whimpering outside. She opened the door and saw Nick on the stoop outside, ready and waiting to escort her home.

Home.

That word, a word that used to conjure such warm and cozy feelings, sounded so sad to her, now. Who knew how expensive that floor repair would be, and how long it would take? She had a feeling she wouldn't have a real home for a long time.

"Sorry, bub," she said to her fox, letting him inside. "But I guess this place is our home for now. Come on in. I think I have something in the fridge for you to eat."

She went to the back of the building, where she checked on all the animals, including the bunnies, giving them their evening care. A couple of them had opened their eyes and were interested in the formula. That was a good sign. And now they looked very comfortable. She gave Bruno a couple of badly needed extra cuddles, as usual, and turned out the light.

Audrey may have forgotten her toothbrush, but she hadn't totally lost her mind. She went back into the break room and pulled out her leftover soup. Lacking coins for the vending machine or anything resembling silverware, she had to resort to a plastic fork and a paper cup of tepid tap water. Luckily, she found an apple in the back of the mostly empty fridge for Nick.

"So," she said to him as she sat down to eat. Because she hadn't eaten much all day, her appetite had returned. She crumbled a few crackers into the soup. "This isn't so bad, is it?"

He was too busy with his apple to answer.

"I think it's really going to be great in here. I can feel it. I mean, this is like heaven, right? Me and a slew of pets. I always dreamed of a life like this, growing up."

Nick licked his paws, uninterested.

Then she went to the front reception area and tried to arrange the plastic chairs in the waiting area into something similar to a bed. She failed magnificently. The chairs were stiff and hard as rocks. Not to mention that she slipped all over in them. Fine for waiting fifteen minutes in, but definitely not okay for sleeping in.

If she were in Piazza Tre right now, she'd have her pillows propped up against the wall and would be watching something on Netflix on her laptop computer, gradually slipping toward dreamland with a nice cup of tea. Trying to capture that sense of home, she opened her laptop and turned on some old medical drama. She didn't have any tea, but she had a bottle of water.

She kept shifting in the pleather seats, trying to get comfortable as she watched. She wasn't big, but her body hung off of them. Finally, after sliding off one and spilling her drink on her T-shirt, she gave up, pillowed some freshly washed dog bedding from the supply closet, and laid it out on the cold tile, among the chairs.

A little better, she thought as she settled in, Nick curled beside her, and started to get interested in the television show.

Just as the medical drama started to heat up, a long, lone howl sounded from the back of the clinic. Nick jumped up, ears perked.

Romeo, the Golden Retriever mix. He was a surrender from a family who'd moved, and he'd been spoiled a lot, so he was a bit of a drama queen. Planning to ignore it, she raised the volume on her computer. As she started to doze off, the sound came again.

And then it was joined by another high-pitched yelp. Sounded like Pip, the Pomeranian. And then, even poor Bruno started to join in.

As she pressed the volume button to raise it again, the back room erupted in the loudest, most grating cacophony of sounds she'd ever heard. She might as well have run in there and announced feeding time.

Suddenly, a howl much closer by erupted behind her.

She groaned, rolled over, and looked at Nick, wagging a warning finger at him. "Now don't you start."

Jumping to her feet, she went to the back room to check on the animals. They all seemed fine. "Okay. Quiet now," she said, giving them all a few extra pets. She gave Romeo an especially long one, since he seemed the most agitated.

But the second she turned out the light, they started again. Louder, this time, so loud it drowned out the television show, even on top volume.

Romeo, Romeo, we know wherefore thou art. In fact, all of Sicily knows, now.

She turned off the laptop and burrowed under the covers, hoping she was so tired she'd fall asleep, no matter what.

But Audrey was wrong. As she lay there in the darkness, staring at the ceiling and listening to the howls of the animals, feeling the hardness of the floor against her back, she made a firm resolution.

She had to fix that floor in her house. Sooner, rather than later. Before she went insane.

*

Audrey woke before daybreak, but as she sat up, she wasn't really sure she'd slept much at all.

The clock in the reception area was a loud one, so loud she could hear its ticking above the animals' whimpers and howls, and she'd started counting ticks of it. She remembered the moment when the animals finally quieted down, because she'd gotten to about ten thousand by the time it happened. By then, a finnicky streetlight outside, slashing through the blinds, had stopped flickering and turned off for good. Then, she'd counted about nine thousand more ticks, all the while staring up at the ceiling and watching the headlights from an occasional passing car making shapes on it.

Maybe she'd fallen asleep then, but she wasn't sure. As she sat up and stretched, she felt like the dead. But she knew she wasn't dead, because the pain was too intense. Her body was sore from head to toe.

"Ughhhh," she moaned as she tried to pull herself up, struggling and grasping onto chairs to help her. She felt twice her age as she limped to the break room to make herself a cup of coffee. As she did, a thought came to her, pretty clearly, above all the others:

I can NOT do that again. I will die, pure and simple.

Once she started a pot brewing, she went into the bathroom. There was no shower, so she had to do her best, washing up at the basin. She did a little bit of a cat wash, wetting paper towels and using them to get as clean as possible before slipping into the new clothes she'd brought. She found a small bottle of mouthwash in the medicine cabinet and used that to get rid of her morning breath. Then she stared at the horror that was her hair.

"It's totally not fair to have bedhead without the bed!" she muttered to herself as she tried to tame her locks with the brush she'd brought. Instead, she had to settle for a low ponytail. It didn't help much. She had dark circles under her eyes and not only felt like the dead, she *looked* like it, too.

"Okay! Time to start the day!" she said cheerfully, grabbing her coffee and taking a sip. As she went to the kennel to check out the animals, her phone started to buzz in her pocket. It was Brina.

"What time is it where you are? Did I wake you?" she asked when Audrey answered.

"It's six. And no, you didn—"

"Morning or night?"

"Morning."

"I don't really care," she interrupted. "Seeing as you call me in the middle of the night *constantly*."

"True. But you're usually up, feeding Byron, right?"

"I'll have you know that Byron started sleeping through the night two weeks ago."

"Really?" Audrey didn't know whether to feel happy or sad about that. As much as she'd rushed to get out of America, there were so many things she missed. Her nieces and nephews, among them. They were growing so fast. Brina posted pictures on her Instagram account, but Audrey rarely had time to look at those. "Why didn't you tell me?"

"I didn't know you needed a play-by-play. And you've been so busy. But that's okay. How are things going? I've been waiting for you to call. Your last message was like, one word. So tell me, what happened?"

She sighed. What had happened with G was the smallest of her disasters right now. She decided to play like it didn't matter, only because with everything else going on, it almost didn't. "Oh, it's no big deal. It wasn't a date. He had a bunch of people over there, tasting, too. So whatever."

"You're disappointed."

Audrey looked up at the ceiling. And here, she thought she'd done a good job at playing nonchalant about it. But it must've been an Older Sister Sixth Sense, because Brina could somehow always sense her emotions, even an ocean away. "No, I'm really not. It's fine."

"No, it's not fine. I can tell from your voice."

"Really, it is. He's probably not the person for me, anyway. He's so confident and outgoing and we live totally different lives. Besides, I have bigger fish to fry at this moment."

"I hope those fish involve one sexy Southerner with abs you can bounce quarters off of?"

"No," she muttered. "You know that's not going to happen, Mason being Mason, and well … perfect. And in fact, I'll have you know, my fish aren't men at all. But I'm taking care of it. I just got a little notice that my place isn't fit for occupancy, and so I had to get out last night. I slept in the clinic."

"You what?" Brina paused. "Oh, my god, Audrey. Are you serious? Why? What's wrong with your house? Is it like, infested with cockroaches?"

"No. No, of course not."

"What, is the roof about to cave in?"

Audrey bristled. "Yeah, I mean, that's pretty close, actually. The floor, if you want to be specific about it."

"And you were sleeping there, in a condemned property?" Mom-Brina suddenly kicked in, and now Audrey felt like one of her kids. Audrey and Brina's mom had always been pretty hands-off, busy with her career. As a mom, Brina had gone the opposite way, turning into the casserole-baking, always-there helicopter type.

"Oh, stop. Really, it isn't that bad. But out of an abundance of caution …"

" … You're sleeping on the street. That's cautious."

"No. I had the clinic."

"Okay. So you're sleeping with the dogs. Much better."

"Ha-ha." She rubbed her sore hip, which ached numbly. "It's not a big deal. I'm going to get it fixed, and everything will be fine. I'm lucky I have this place, or I *would* be out on the street."

"Stop. Just let me wire you some money and go stay in a hotel."

"I don't need—"

"Oh, stop playing the martyr."

"No. You've already sent me enough money, and I'm going to pay you back for that. I don't need any more. I'm fine."

Brina said something about how she wished Audrey would stop being so stubborn, but just then, someone knocked on the door, and Audrey didn't catch all of it. She checked the time on the clock. It was indeed six in the morning, three hours before opening.

"Hey, Brina? I have to call you back. Someone's at the door," she said, walking into the reception area.

It was dark there because she'd closed the blinds in the front of the building so she could get some sleep, but early-morning sun was just starting to outline the windows. She ended the call and unlocked the door, half-expecting to see some do-gooder with another cardboard box of poor strays. Hopefully, no more bunnies.

Instead, she saw Mr. Cascarelli. He was standing there, looking very much like his beloved pet had just died. "I'm sorry to bother you so early, Dottore Smart, but I have a very full day on my hands and I saw your light on."

Oh, what a sweet man, she thought, smiling at him. *He's come to say that he's sorry for yesterday.*

"It's fine!" she said to him, pushing aside the door to let him in. As she did, she realized she hadn't picked up the shambles that was her makeshift bed.

He saw it at the same moment. "Oh!" he moaned, as if it were a terrible tragedy. "You slept *there?*"

"Yes, but it was fine! I'm lucky I had this place. No harm done." She motioned him in and pointed to her mug. "Coffee?"

He shook his head and cleared his throat, unable to meet her eyes, guilty. "Dottore Smart, I—"

"Please. There's really no need to apologize. I understand how these things go. You were just doing your—"

His eyes widened and he said, "Uh, no. I'm not here to apologize," he said, scanning the place. "I am here to do the inspection. I am sure I told you about it yesterday? Remember?"

She stared at him for a moment, mouth open, and in that brief moment, her entire life flashed before her eyes. "Oh. This early?"

"Yes. I'm sorry. I know it is early, but I have a long list of homes to look over today."

"Oh. Well, that's fine." She motioned around her. "Then by all means, inspect."

She feigned confidence, but inside, it felt like every nerve she had was being plucked like a banjo.

But please please please don't find anything bad!

CHAPTER SIX

Audrey walked behind the inspector silently, as if treading on eggshells. She had all of her fingers crossed behind her back. Nick followed, too, like the caboose of the train, not wanting to be left out.

Suddenly, the horrible night's sleep she had on the lobby floor seemed like a dream compared to the thoughts going through her head—getting shooed from a supermarket doorway for squatting too long, covering herself with newspapers, climbing into an old dumpster to stay warm … she'd always had compassion for the homeless, giving them her spare change when she passed them on the street. She'd never once thought that could be *her* life.

Her nerves were so tight that every time he turned around to ask a simple question, she nearly jumped back as if he'd jabbed her with a cattle prod. Then he'd look at her like she was up to no good.

"Dottore Smart, you say you engaged a contractor for these renovations?"

She nodded. "Yes. Mason Legare. You might know him. You performed an inspection on his house the other—"

There was a decidedly deep frown on his face when he said, "Legare? Oh, yes, I do remember him. On Via Milano. The one with the railing."

She might as well have said she'd gotten help from the devil. *Great, Mason. Making friends in all the right places, are you?*

"Yes, that's right. Anyway, he helped with a lot of the work here," she said, wondering if she should've kept Mason's name out of it. "But I did a lot of it on my own, too."

"Mmmhmm," he said, continuing on his inspection.

Great. So now we're back to mmmhmms again.

He stopped at one of the dog kennels to pet an excited pooch, who wagged its tail adoringly. Audrey knew that animals were the best judges of character there were, so if this dog liked Mr. Cascarelli, he couldn't be all that bad. "Cute little pup," he said with a smile. "What's his name?"

"Oh. That's Alfonzo. We think he's a poodle-terrier mix? He's a little scoundrel," she said, leaning against the wall. "Have you ever considered adopting?"

He stood up and shook his head sadly. "Would have loved to. Not now. Too much going on. My new place doesn't allow pets, either."

Audrey shrugged. "Oh well. If you ever change your mind or decide to move, you know where we are! We have quite the selection here."

"I see that. And the place is very clean. The bones of the place are old, but you've done well. The animals seem to be well taken care of. Of course, our health inspector will need to make sure about that. I'm only here to comment on the building itself."

"Of course. I understand."

She led him to the bathroom. He peeked in, turned on a light, flushed the toilet, ran the water, and nodded, satisfied. She brought him down the hall to her office, the two storage rooms, and then the final room in the back, the break room. He inspected everything closely, then marked something on his clipboard.

"And that's the end of the tour," she said with a shrug. "It's pretty small."

He kept writing. "You say you opened …"

"Just last month."

"Good. Looks good," he said to Audrey's relief. "Just need to make a few—"

He stopped suddenly and craned his neck, like he was looking or listening for something.

"What's that?"

Oh no, she thought, following his line of vision. *This was when the floor dropped out from under me the last time. Almost literally.*

But all she saw there was the door to the back alley. She'd been through that door, only to drop the garbage into the dumpster there. "Oh. That's just egress to the alley in back. I only go out there to toss out the trash. I didn't think you needed to—"

He began to storm off in that direction like a man on a mission, as fast as his stubby legs would carry him. He pushed open the door and made his way through, then looked around, confused, as if he expected to see something that wasn't there.

"Yeah, it's just an exit, like I said." She pushed open the door to the outside to show him that it was in working order. "I didn't think—"

"I'm looking for an opening for a crawl space. All the buildings in this area have them. Do you—" He stopped when he saw something behind the door and rushed to it. "Aha."

Audrey stared at the big wood-outlined panel. It blended almost invisibly into the wall. She hadn't even noticed that was there. "We don't use that," she said.

"Still …" he said, turning the ancient catch on it. Paint flecked off as he pried the cover off the opening, indicating that it hadn't been opened since it'd been painted. When he slipped the lid off, a musty, cold breeze that smelled a little like copper, garbage, and moldy death wafted out. She felt like an archaeologist, unearthing a tomb of some long-dead pharaoh. That couldn't be good. Didn't curses come with disturbing things like this?

Audrey waved a hand in front of her nose as he pulled a giant flashlight from his belt and switched it on. He stooped, and so did she, straining to see.

"What even *is* that?" she asked.

"A lot of these old places have them. For the plumbing and electrical."

"Oh."

He got on his hands and knees and started to disappear inside, but stopped while his feet were still outside of the crawl space. "Uh-oh."

She winced. That definitely wasn't good. "What?"

"Oh no. Oh no. Oh no no no no no no no no …" he wailed, making her wonder whether he'd encountered the ghost of his dead mother down there.

She leaned over and tried to peer inside, but the smell nearly suffocated her. It seemed even worse now. As she held her nose and moved closer, a giant black spider the size of her fist crawled out along the edge of the frame, making her jump. Okay. No way on Earth was she *ever* going in or anywhere near that hole again. No way. "What?"

"You have black mold. Quite a lot of it."

Mold? Was that all? Hardly seemed like anything to get upset over. The mutant spider from hell had seemed way worse. "Oh. Is that serious?"

He backed out of the crawl space and shut the flashlight off. "Yes. It can be dangerous." He climbed to his feet and started to scribble something on his clipboard again. "Very dangerous."

"You mean like, a silent killer? Like carbon monoxide?"

40

"Oh, no. Not quite that level. But it still can cause grave health problems."

"Okay. But can't we just like … scrape it off?" *Or hire someone else to scrape it off since … dark, black hole with insanely large spiders.* Either way, it didn't seem like that much of a dealbreaker.

"No. It's more serious than that. Toxic mold is, well … toxic," he muttered, still writing. She peered over edge of the clipboard and saw that same harsh, red lettering she remembered from the last slip of paper.

Oh no no no no no no no … .

"Wait," Audrey said, sure this was a repeat of what happened yesterday, only in a different location. "Are you saying you're closing the clinic down?"

"I don't see any choice," he murmured, more to the paper than to her. Then he tore something off and …

No. This isn't happening. I refuse to let this happen. This is nothing but a bad dream. That's it, I'm not sleeping well, and I'm not in my own bed, so I'm hallucinating.

She tried pinching herself. That didn't wake her up.

"But … I have dozens of animals! They'll be out on the street again. The city wouldn't want that."

"I'm sorry, but you'll have to take that up with them."

She thought of Councilman Falco, her friend on the board. He could help, but usually everything he did was a matter of taking things in front of the board, getting an ordinance. The bureaucracy was layers deep. Nothing he did for her ever happened overnight. Plus, despite giving the elected official's standard speech about how she "could always count on" him, he was notoriously absent from her life. "I wouldn't know what to …" She froze.

Oh, god, Brina's right. I'm going to be living on the street, fighting for newspapers to keep myself warm and looking for spare dumpsters to crawl into to protect me from the elements. Me and all the strays.

He ripped the paper off the clipboard and held it in front of her. She didn't know what the Italian words written in red said, but they taunted her anyway. It was the same as the last one. Audrey pressed her lips together, trying to stifle the sob in her throat. She succeeded.

He didn't. His mouth suddenly opened and he let out a wail. "I'm so sorry. All those animals!"

41

For a beat, she just stared at him. It was so sudden and pronounced, it almost seemed like a farce. Was he making fun of her? She looked closer. No … those were definite tears in the corners of his eyes.

"Hey, hey, hey, it's all right," she said, taking his arm and leading him to a chair in the break room. She filled a cup of water for him. He gulped it greedily as she looked around for a tissue. She found some paper towels and handed them to him. He dabbed his eyes and blew his nose loudly. "Take a deep breath. You're going to be all right."

"I'm sorry," he blubbered, shaking his head. "It doesn't feel all right. I don't want to be the bad guy. But I'm always the bad guy. People see me coming and run inside."

"You're not. Like I said before, you're just doing your job."

He sniffled like a little boy. "Ha. Not well enough, according to the city government."

"What do you mean?"

"They say I'm no good. I was. Before, it was okay. But someone high up in the government, maybe the mayor, thinks that if word gets out about all these inexperienced home renovators living in these places, fixing them up, there might be injuries. Damages. Lawsuits. They say it's happened before, in other countries, and they're afraid of it happening here and bankrupting the town. So they put pressure on me to put pressure on all the foreigners coming here. To be tough. To be hard. To do make sure they do everything exactly up to code. No cut corners." His accent seemed thicker now, and then he dissolved into some Italian she didn't understand. He shook his head and pounded his fist on his thigh. "But I feel terrible, kicking all these people out of their homes. I've done five in the last two days. Five. People with families. Kids. Little money."

Audrey's heart squeezed in her chest. The guy was clearly having a bad day. A bad week. Maybe even a bad life. She patted his shoulder. "Don't worry. It's not your fault. Everybody knows that."

He pouted. "No, they don't. The last woman I gave a slip to told me she hopes I rot in hell with the other devils."

"Oh," Audrey said. Had Mr. Cascarelli been a jerk, she might've resorted to similar language. She wondered if Mason had called him anything colorful from his extensive Southern vocabulary. "Well, *almost* everybody knows that."

He didn't seem cheered by that. Instead, he said, "The black mold is dangerous, and it might take time to remove, but it shouldn't affect the

42

pets in those front rooms. So they can stay. But I can't have you living here or seeing patients in here. I get in trouble."

She nodded. "Thank you. I understand."

"Black mold is tricky, but not too hard. You can probably do the remove yourself with the right tools. Very inexpensive. As soon as you get it out of there, call me directly at the number on the form. I will come back and pass you right away."

"Okay. Yes. That's great. Thank you."

She walked him out to the front of the building, laughing to herself. *He failed me, and I'm thanking him?* But with the way he hung his head and seemed about to break out into tears again when he passed the kennels suggested he was about one step away from losing it. She decided to handle him with kid gloves, just like one of her injured animals.

"Please. Don't you worry about me. I'll be fine. I'm a tough one," she said as she saw him out the door.

"Are you sure?" he asked, turning back to her, tears still threatening to spill.

"Quite sure," she said, nodding at him as she closed the door.

Then she looked back at the pile of blankets, last night's sleeping arrangements, and her body started to ache again. She rubbed her aching muscles and yawned. *I think.*

Two huge renovations. Lots of money. Lots of stress. As if I don't have enough of that. My business is closed, and unless I can start getting money in soon, I'm going to be in huge trouble! Not to mention that I don't have a place to sleep tonight. How am I going to do this without going insane?

Suddenly, her father's words occurred to her. *One thing at a time is all we can do.*

Right. What was the most pressing item on the list? The most vital? Finding a place to sleep that night. Definitely.

At that moment, an idea popped into her head, one that would be better than sleeping out on the streets.

Marginally, at least.

CHAPTER SEVEN

The next time Audrey saw Mason, she was not prepared.

It was nearly midday, and yet he was wearing plaid pajama pants, loose on his slim waist, and, of course, shirtless. He must've forgotten to pack enough T-shirts when he moved here from Charleston, because he almost *never* seemed to be wearing one.

Especially when she was at her weakest, like now. She already felt dizzy and tired. Now, she was completely lightheaded.

"Hi," she said, covering for her bulging eyes by snapping them shut and adding in an extended yawn as she stood on the stoop of the well-appointed corner home on via Milano.

Mason stared down at her, that same bewitching smirk on his face that made her want to kiss and punch him at the same time. "What the heck happened to you? Shouldn't you be at work?"

Yes, she'd seen better days, days when she didn't bathe in a sink, her grooming ritual had at least included brushing her teeth, and she wasn't carrying all the clothing she owned on her back. Thinking of her failed inspection, she glanced at the railing that Cascarelli had dinged Mason on. It looked absolutely perfect.

Which only meant this whole inspection racket was probably a crock. A crock meant to milk every last cent from the well-meaning expats who moved here.

The thought made her even angrier.

"Thanks. Yeah, I should be. It's a long story. Can I come in?" ... *And call this my home for the foreseeable future?*

He shrugged and waved her in. She stepped in to the aroma of something close to bacon. Despite what those abs would suggest, Mason didn't eat like a bodybuilder. He was a true meat-and-potatoes kind of guy, the kind of man who couldn't count a calorie to save his life. He'd made her dinner, once, and though delicious, it wasn't exactly easy on the hips. Came from his Southern upbringing.

As she walked in with Nick, he started his hissing again. Polpetto barked.

"Oh, stop it, you two," she growled, on her last nerve.

"Whoa. Bad day?"

"Yeah. You could say that." She had to admit, everything about Mason's sunny little house was so perfect, it made her a little jealous. "Aw, is momma making one of little Mason's favorite home-cooked meals?" she asked as she looked around his bright hallway.

"*Momma* is gone," he said, motioning her through to the kitchen. "I dropped her off at the airport yesterday. This is *my* specialty."

"Oh," she said as he stuffed his hand in an oven mitt and opened the tiny oven. *That's actually ... perfect.* "What is it?"

"Biscuits and gravy. I'll tell you, after my momma left I had a hankering for the stuff. Don't know why," he said, pulling out some perfectly browned biscuits and setting them on the stovetop. "Made it with Italian sausage so who knows what it's like. I know it ain't fancy like your boyfriend makes, but there's enough for two."

On the rug under the tiny kitchen table that was too small to serve as a tent for him, Polpetto whined.

"Sorry, boy. Enough for three."

It was on the tip of her tongue to tell him G wasn't her boyfriend, but Audrey decided to ignore it for now. It didn't matter anyway. "Thanks. I'd love that. It sounds great. Can I help?"

"No. Just sit your butt there. It'll be ready in a minute."

She threw her heavy bag to the ground with a huff, stretched her aching back, and went to pet Polpetto, who wagged his tail excitedly. The second she did, Nick growled, wanting her all to himself. "Stop it. There is plenty of me to go around."

"Yeah. I find myself saying that all the time." Mason must not have noticed the giant bag on her back before, because when he turned back, he said, "You girls don't exactly travel light, do you?"

"Well, to tell you the truth, I know it's only noon, but I've had a bit of a bad d—bad week, actually. As of the last time I saw you."

He stopped what he was doing, grabbed a cask of red wine, and poured her a glass, which he set in front of her. Despite being self-obsessed most of the time, Mason did have his bright, shining moments. "What happened? Did your chef friend's desserts disappoint?"

"What? Oh, no." God, her non-date with G seemed like a thousand years ago. But of course, Mason would focus in on that. He seemed to love ribbing her on her non-existent love life.

"Then what?"

45

"Yesterday, I had a little visit from the inspector. At my house," she grumbled, wrapping her hands around the glass. "And then today, I had another one. At the clinic."

He turned away from the stove, where he was plating the biscuits, eyebrow raised. "Told you that guy was a jerk. I would've wrung his neck if it weren't the size of the Mississippi."

"Oh, he's not. He's a big sweetheart!"

He chuckled. "Yeah, right. He gave the same little love note to Rob and Dominic down the street. You know those guys?"

She shook her head. "Who?"

"They're good guys. Expats just like you and me. But now they're scrambling like you are, rooming in some fleabag hotel until they can get repairs made, on account of that scumbag."

As much as it made her feel better to know she wasn't alone, she still felt bad for the inspector. Audrey had a job people respected. It couldn't be easy having a job that made people cringe when they saw you coming. "He is not a scumbag! Like I said, he's a sweetheart."

"Okay. Whatever you say. I seem to remember you saying the same thing about Polpetto, too, and the creature ate my favorite boots."

Audrey laughed. "He did?"

Mason shot Polpetto some eye daggers. "Shut it. You know I've owned those boots since I was eighteen? I thought they were dang near indestructible."

"Then I think you need new ones."

"You don't get it. You don't understand the relationship a Southern man has with his boots. Once you break 'em in, ain't nothing more valuable."

She fully admitted she didn't get it, as was the case with most of the things that came out of his mouth. "I'm sorry. That is a true tragedy." She rubbed her hands together. "But ... on to more important topics. Do you think that this is all part of some elaborate scheme to get us foreigners paying way more than we expected for our renovations, and to bolster the economy?"

"I think you're giving these country people a little too much credit. My neighbor to the right? Lived here all his life and didn't even know what the internet was. And he's on the city council. This ain't some vast Mussomeli government conspiracy."

He came over to her with a plate. On it were two biscuits, split open, covered with some pale gray, lumpy gravy. No, it didn't look as appetizing as G's creations, but she wasn't about to tell him that. The man had cooked her lunch. She could've kissed him.

He sat down across from her. "So, long story short, the inspector revoked your CO?"

She nodded as she took a forkful of food, blew on it, and nibbled a bite.

Despite the way it looked, it was *fantastic*. She quickly loaded her fork again. "This is really good."

He shrugged like he already knew that. "That blows. Which place?"

"Both."

"Both, you mean … *both*?" He stopped with his fork halfway between the plate and his mouth. Part of it dripped off. "Wow, girl. I get the house. That's all jacked up. But the clinic? I worked on all that. What in God's name is wrong with the clinic?"

"Hey. The house isn't that much of a hot mess," she said defensively. "But apparently, there's black mold in the clinic."

"Black mold? Where?"

"In the crawl space."

"What crawl space?"

"*Exactly!* I didn't even know there was one! But nevertheless. It's spore central. *Toxic* spore central. Can kill you while you sleep."

"Eh, bull. Little black mold never killed no one," he said.

"Really? Is it easy to remove? The inspector seemed to think it was."

Somehow, he'd managed to shovel all that food into his mouth, while she was only on her third bite. His plate was empty, practically licked clean. "Not that easy. Not hard, either. You need the right tools. And it'll probably cost you, even if you do it yourself. But it shouldn't take too long."

"It's expensive? The inspector seemed to think—"

"The inspector seems to think a lot of things, none of which are all that bright. It'll cost for the supplies. And it could be a pain, if you don't get it all … it's just gonna come back and then you'll have the same issue six months from now."

"I'd probably hire an expert. But see, the problem is, I don't—"

"Have the money. I know. You don't *ever* have the money."

It was true. Most of the repairs she wanted to make, she had to hold off on because of lack of funds. Though she'd withdrawn most of her nest egg for the move, it'd been spent pretty quickly upon arrival in Mussomeli. The promise of making more had always been there,

47

though, once the clinic opened. But it hadn't been opened nearly long enough. Business at the clinic might've been good, but the start-up expenses had been pretty steep. And now ... another wrench. "Right. And I'm not doing it myself. Spiders."

He shot her an amused look. "I thought you loved all God's creatures, Boston."

"Not spiders."

"Ah. Wuss."

"Shut up. You were the one who cried the first time you had to clean up Polpetto's turds."

He ignored her. "So it'll probably run you a couple thousand euros. But shouldn't the city be footing the bill for a repair like this?"

She shook her head. "I called Falco before I came over here. He told me that pitiful little allowance he gave me when I first started the reno was supposed to cover things like this and they couldn't find any more money in the budget, so I'm on my own. But I guess this is an emergency. And the inspector did say that once I made the changes, he'd come right back and pass it."

"Wow, you are on his good side. He could give two farts about me. I was sure he wanted to fail me, just for the sheer pleasure of it. I think it gave him physical pain to put the APPROVED stamp on my papers."

He rifled through a stack of them on the table and showed her the certificate, which a bright, shiny stamp on it. If *she'd* had one of those, she'd frame it.

"Well ... that's because you're annoying as anything," she said, sipping her wine.

"Really?" He pushed his empty plate away and placed his elbows on the table, his chin resting in his hands. "So tell me. I'm curious. How am I ... the guy who just invited you in out of the cold, th—"

"It's sixty-five degrees out."

"Whatever. The guy who fed you, gave you drink and his famous Southern hospitality ... how is he annoying, again?"

She shrugged. "Did you feed *him*?" When he stared at her, clearly taken off guard by the question, she added, "Maybe you should've. Maybe it would've put you on his good side."

"Sorry. I got my stamp. Besides, I prefer my dining company to be a little better looking," he said with a wink, wiping his mouth and standing up. He grabbed Polpetto's dog dish and ladled a dose of gravy over his kibble. Audrey decided to spare him the lecture on dogs eating

48

human food, because a rather preteen-ish thought went through her head right then. *Hee, he thinks I'm pretty.*

No, Audrey. He said you were better looking than an overweight, balding, middle-aged man with a double chin. This is not exactly a win.

"So what are you going to do now?" he asked, sitting back down and popping open one of his favorite Sicilian beers. "What about all the strays? Where are they? You have to move them out now?"

"Oh. He said they could stay in the clinic, but that I couldn't see patients there. Basically, humans aren't allowed in there except to care for the animals, until the problem has been taken care of."

"Oh. Okay. So … again. What are you going to do?"

"Oh, well …" She looked down at her bag. "I cancelled all of next week's appointments. I have the weekend off, so I'm going to figure it out then. Probably start calling specialists in to help and see if I can get a loan so I can get the mold taken care of."

"But what about *you*?"

She knew what he was asking, and yes, she'd been putting it off. She'd hoped that he would just offer, without her having to lay it on the line. But unfortunately, Mason was thick, or he just liked making women beg. Whatever it was, she just had to bite the bullet and get it out. "Well, I don't really have the money for a hotel, so …"

He nodded, then said, very seriously, "Geez. That sucks. So what street are you sleeping on?"

She waited a beat for him to say he was just kidding. But he didn't. He really was going to milk this, the jerk.

Instead, he kept on with it. "I hear Via Bengasi has great views of the sunrise. Or if you stay in Piazza Roma, you can always get a square of pavement near the fountain, if you watch out for the pigeon poop. Just don't stay outside *my* place. The last thing I need is property values going—"

She leaned over and smacked him on his hard, well-shaped bicep.

"Ow!" he said, like a total baby, rubbing his arm. "All right, all right, cut it out. You know I was just kidding with you. You can stay in my guest room while you figure things out. I'm going to be gone all day tomorrow anyway, so my place is yours."

The guest room. The thought of sleeping upstairs, so close to him, sent a little shiver through her. "Thanks. But I don't even need the guest room. Your sofa is fine."

He eyed her with a bit of confusion.

"I mean … if you make me too comfortable, I might never want to move out. So …"

"All right. Suit yourself. Whatever you want." He leaned forward, a serious look on his face. "But what I want to know is, if you needed a place to stay, why didn't you go to that boyfriend of yours?"

That was the million-dollar question. She really didn't know. It wasn't even about the date-that-wasn't-a-date. It should've been easier to go to him as a friend, and he would've gladly put her up in his place over the café. But for some reason, the second she'd thought about a place to stay, she'd thought about Mason. G hadn't even come to mind.

Why? She couldn't answer that.

"For the last time, he's not my boyfriend," she said to him, bringing her wine to her lips and taking a sip. "He's just a friend."

"Whatever you say. You know, I have some—not a lot, but some—experience with black mold. I can probably fix it for you, if you play your cards right."

He wiggled his eyebrows. She stuck her tongue out like she was going to be sick.

"I could. That way, you wouldn't have to take out that loan you were talking about."

"No, really. I couldn't let you do that. I'd feel—"

"All right. Then pay me when you're able to. When the clinic starts doing better. I don't like the idea of those animals marinating in that situation, same as you. I may be annoying, but I ain't heartless. So just let me do it. All right?"

He seemed so resolute, she simply couldn't say no. Since when had he become her knight in shining armor? "I guess. At least I should let you take a look at it first and see what you think. It might be too big a job for you."

"Good deal." He took a gulp of his beer. "So you have off all day tomorrow?"

"Well, yes. I have to go in and take care of the strays, but—"

"I'm taking the day off, going to Agrigento to see the ruins. Haven't gotten a chance to get down there. You ever been?"

She shook her head. She'd wanted to. It was supposed to be amazing and historic, with beautiful temples of the gods. At one point, she'd planned a trip down there, but a little thing like being a suspect in a murder had stopped her from leaving the city limits. Now was not the time to be sightseeing, though. She had thousands of things to do, the least of which was figuring out how to make her properties livable again.

"You should come along. Get away. You look stressed."

She let out a wistful sigh at the thought. Yes, she was starting to feel burned out, and it wasn't just the lack of sleep from the previous night. The distraction would be welcome, but it wasn't exactly the responsible thing to do. "That sounds nice, but I really should—"

"Come on. When was the last time you didn't have to work? Plus, if I'm gonna do the work on the place, you're gonna have to wait for me to come back anyway."

"I don't know. The animals need me, and I should—"

"Get that kid of yours—that Luca—to look after them. It's just for a day. He's reliable, right?"

She nodded. "He is, but—"

"And if you want to stop in in the morning to look in on them, I'll check out the mold situation then. All right?"

"Well … I really should—"

"You *should* do a lot of things, and that's all you've been doing. Do something you *want* to do, for once," he said, his blue eyes boring into hers in a way that made her entire body heat up like a flame.

Stop it, body. He's just a crush. Totally unattainable. Remember?

But she'd gotten away once, months ago, to go to Catania on the coast, and that had completely refreshed her, giving her hope and that little nudge to carry on. That was something G had told her: *You cannot escape your problems by running from them. You can press pause on them for a bit. Take them on when you are in a better frame of mind.*

So, looking into his eyes, feeling a shiver travel from her head to her toes, she nodded slightly. "All right. Let's do it."

CHAPTER EIGHT

Mason had the biggest, fluffiest, most wonderful couch.

She wouldn't tell that to him, though, because he likely already knew it. The guy thought he had the most wonderful *everything*.

She smiled as she opened her eyes and stretched in the sunny yellow living room with the lovely ivy plants outside climbing up the trellis of the window. She'd had such a restful night's sleep, she wished she could bottle it and open it every night. It was one of those sleeps where she'd fallen so deeply that she could barely remember it at all. She'd been a rock.

Before she could untangle herself from the blanket, though, Polpetto, who, though he was the size of a truck, still seemed to think he was a puppy, clambered in, jumping on her mid-section and whooshing all the air out of her lungs. Nick was on his tail.

"Uh!" she mumbled breathlessly. "Help!"

It only got worse when Nick joined in. She really thought she was going to die from the sheer weight.

"Hey. She's our guest. Don't kill her," Mason's voice called from the arched doorway as Audrey's arms and legs flailed underneath the weight of the animals. He snapped his fingers.

Polpetto reluctantly jumped off, leaving Audrey panting, her hair a staticky revolt upon her head. Nick lingered on her chest proudly, as if to say, *I win.* Of course, Mason was fully dressed and looking just as scrumptious as ever. He held a mug in front of him. "Espresso?"

She smoothed down her hair as she nudged Nick away and pulled off the blanket. Then, when she realized she was wearing her *It's all Fun and Games Until Someone Winds Up in a Cone* T-shirt and peach-butt boxers, pulled it back up again. "Yes, that would be lovely."

He seemed to catch sight of them anyway, because he smirked a little. She jumped off of the couch before the dastardly pet duo could launch another attack and followed him into the kitchen, where he handed her a steaming cup, then sat down in his chair. "Bought fresh bread from Pepe if you want a slice."

She nodded.

He slathered a chunk of bread in butter and handed it to her. She took a nibble. Still warm and delicious; she let out an *mmmm* of approval.

"Sleep well?"

"Amazing." She took a sip of the espresso. Of course, his espresso was amazing. Did anything this guy do *not* turn out awesome? She could get used to this.

"Shower's upstairs, first door on your right. Left a couple towels out for you."

Aw. That was so cute. And impressive. Was that what he was trying to do … impress his guest? Or did he normally do this for everyone? She licked her fingers. "Thanks. You keep treating me this well and I might want to make this permanent."

He frowned. "What do you mean? Ain't doing nothing special."

Oh. Right. His life was normally this special. Wasn't that how it was usually for the beautiful people?

When she polished off her bread, he was back to regular Mason. "I want to get out of here at eight, and I know you want to stop by the clinic, so don't take too long, Boston."

She smiled and set the mug down, then stood up. "Fine. But I want to stop by the hardware store, too, and leave a spare key with Luca so he can walk the dogs for me and I can show him how to feed the bunnies."

He let out a sigh. "Five minutes."

"Stop being so bossy."

"My house. My rules," he muttered after her.

*

Agrigento was only forty-five minutes away by car, near the southern coast of Sicily and on the Mediterranean. Audrey knew all this because of the plans she'd once made to go there, but back then, she'd been hoping to interview a witness to clear her of murder, not to sightsee. But *everyone* talked about Agrigento, and how amazing it was.

"So, what are we going to see?" she asked Mason as they sped down the road in his little powder-blue Fiat, Polpetto securely wedged between them in the tight cabin of the little car. "You said ruins?"

He nodded. "Yeah, the Valley of Temples."

"The what?"

"It's a collection of all the temples of the gods, dating back thousands of years. What, have you been living under a rock, girl?"

She shrugged. "I haven't had much free time, you know. Something about renovating a house and building a business from scratch …"

"Right, right. But everyone's heard of these ruins. They're supposed to be incredible."

"Oh. Okay," she said, getting more excited as he pressed on, upshifting on the meandering, winding hills outside the city. As he did, she glanced at his hand, wrapped around the shifter. Tanned, with just the slightest bit of hair, and not a trace of an age spot or unsightly vein. The man could've been a hand model, too.

"Boston, you're just going to have to chill if you want to ride with me," he said.

She glanced over at him. He'd donned his dark sunglasses, which made him look even more beautiful and gave her a giddy, weightless feeling. "I am chill. I'm fine."

"Then stop digging your fingernails into the leather."

She looked down. Yep, she was, her knuckles white. She slowly unfurled her claws into regular hands and laughed. "Sorry. I keep thinking of the clinic. I hope the animals will—"

He reached over and grabbed her hand, which she realized was starting to curl up in a claw again, surprising her so much that her heart stuttered in her chest. "Relax. I told you, I can take care of the mold situation. It ain't that bad. And Luca will look after the animals just fine. Besides, we'll be back by dinnertime."

"Okay. Thanks."

They drove on until the bright blue line of sea appeared in the distance, and the city of Agrigento appeared beneath them. As they descended into the valley, Audrey's ears popping from the elevation change, she started feeling a little less worried, and more excited about the adventure in front of them.

As they drove up to the dirt road leading the ruins, Audrey spied the stone columns and monoliths rising out of the green landscape and let out a gasp. "Look!"

They were spread out upon the whitewashed stone ground, in the sand and dirt. Dozens of temples with impressive columns, the homes of the Gods. When they parked in a lot along with the other tourists, she quickly scrambled out of the car and headed toward an information board. It was in Italian, but that didn't stop her from staring at it, mouth agog. "Did you know that it was this amazing?" she asked breathlessly as a shadow of a person came up behind her.

When Mason didn't answer, she looked and saw an Asian guy in a bucket hat, with a camera, glaring at her, like, *Please get out of my way and stop hogging the sign.*

"Oh, sorry," she said, moving aside to find Mason, who was still trying to wrangle Polpetto out of the car. Apparently, Polpetto wasn't much of a history buff. A shame; Nick had really wanted to go, but Audrey wasn't sure what their policy was on wild animals.

She rushed back to help him. She patted her thighs and said, "Here, Polpy. Come on, baby."

The giant mastiff quickly got to his feet, jumped out, and ran to her.

Mason scowled. "They go to vet school and they think they know everything," he muttered.

"It's called sweet talk!" she said. "You should know, you catch more flies with honey…"

"Yeah, yeah," he muttered, heading up the staircase with his hands in the pockets of his jeans.

She followed him up the steps to a grassy field, studded with rocks and the occasional olive tree. In the distance, a large, crumbling edifice stood, and beyond that, the modern buildings of the city of Agrigento loomed. As they walked toward it, Audrey took out her camera and started snapping photographs.

Mason turned around as she snapped a picture and grinned. "You're taking photos of my butt again, aren't you?"

"Ew. You wish," she said, though she had to admit, it'd probably be nice to get a picture of the two of them together. Her sister would definitely appreciate it. Even if this wasn't a date, she was out doing something she never could do back in the States. Living life. Enjoying herself. That was what she'd flown halfway across the world for, right?

She motioned him closer to her. "Come on. Selfie."

He easily obliged, since he was a big fan of pictures of himself. He wrapped an arm around her, and she held the phone at arm's length, trying to get both of their faces, and a little of the ruins, in the frame.

"No, not like that," he said.

"Like what?"

"Here, let me do it," he said, taking the camera from her. Somehow, he was able to find just the right angle for the photo, so that when he snapped it, she had to admit it was social-media worthy.

"Wow," she said, staring at it. "You're good."

55

He shrugged like it was no big deal, then took Polpetto's leash and led him up another flight of stairs. Audrey hung back and quickly texted the picture to Brina with the caption, *Finally making it to the ruins in Agrigento.*

As she rushed to catch up, her phone buzzed. She looked at the text. *Who cares about a bunch of old dusty buildings. I'm more interested in the MAN!*

She laughed. She knew Brina would say that.

Then a second later, another text appeared: *Nice picture, but would be better with ABS.*

"What's so funny?"

She looked up and realized Mason was standing not five steps from her, gazing curiously at her. She tried to wipe the smile off her face, but just then, she imagined Mason stripping off his T-shirt in the middle of the ruins of the gods, to have a picture taken. *A god among gods.* She couldn't help it. She started to laugh.

"What?" Now he looked more annoyed than anything. "Show me."

Before she could pocket her phone, he grabbed it from her and glanced at the text.

"Ah. Who's Sabrina again? Friend?"

"Sister."

"Yeah?"

"Yes. She and my mom are my only family."

"No dad?"

"Not since I was twelve. He left without a word and I haven't seen or heard from him since. My mother freaks out if I even mention his name."

"Seriously? That's rough." He stared at the text. "So … Brina. Younger, older? Is she hot? This isn't the first time I've caught you texting with her. Why does she like me so much?"

"Don't you mean, 'Obviously she likes me, because what's not to love about me?'"

He shrugged. "Come on. I'm not that big a jerk."

Well, at least he recognized that.

"She's *beautiful*, actually, and two years older, though she looks about ten. She got the sultry vixen looks and I got the cute-as-a-button freckles," Audrey muttered, trying to keep the envy out of her voice. "But she also has three kids and is happily married, so …"

"So I'm her side treat?" The smirk was back. "I could go for that."

Audrey mimed gagging. "You're gross. And believe me, she's *way* too good for you."

He touched the picture of Brina in her profile, studied it, and nodded. "Probably." Then he handed the phone back to her. "What? You sound bitter, Boston. Was there some kind of sibling rivalry going on there?"

"No. Of course not."

"What ... did Daddy like her better?"

"No! In fact, I was always daddy's little girl," she said.

"All right. But ... I don't know. There's some baggage there you're not telling me about. He stroked his chin, staring her down. "Sorry, I'm an only child. I don't get this sibling stuff."

"Brina's my best friend. But ..." She stopped. Was she really going to go into this with him?

"But what? Come on, tell me."

Now he was looking at her, urging it out of her. She got the feeling no woman could look into those blue eyes, pleading with them, and say no. "Well," she said, "Brina is and always has been my best friend. But she's always been the best, the first, at everything. She was the spotlight seeker, and I hated that."

He listened carefully, nodding. "Somehow I don't see you shrinking into the background anywhere."

"It's true, I was the wallflower!" she said, walking away from him so he wouldn't be able to see how much she was blushing. She'd figured Mason for a lot of things, but one thing she hadn't expected him to be was a good listener. "It's always been that way. But Brina? She has her life together. Perfect family, perfect life."

"Your life ain't so bad, is it?" he said, walking along with her, Polpetto by his side.

"No," she said. "Well ... it was."

"*Was?* Why?"

She stopped under the shade of an olive tree, staring at the ruins of one of the biggest temples in the distance. Around them, tourists were milling about, taking photographs, but as gorgeous as it was, and as wonderful the weather was, she suddenly found herself in desolate, cold Boston, dreaming of a way out of her awful apartment, thankless job, go-nowhere love life ... it was a downright dreary existence that made her shiver, even now.

Was she really going to tell him how pathetic her life had been?

Somehow, she couldn't seem to stop herself. "My job was with a bunch of doctors who thought they were better than everyone else. My apartment was a one-room closet, and I couldn't even afford that. And my most meaningful relationship only wanted me for a tumble in a coat closet."

He'd been looking at the ground, but his eyes snapped to hers. "Coat closet?"

"Yeah. I know. Pathetic. And part of me coming out here was wanting to do something different, instead of sitting in Brina's shadow like a totally invisible nobody. Sometimes I think that might even be why I went to vet school. Not because I love animals, but to do something different, so I could at least be seen, for once."

"Ah. Not pathetic. But you're not getting me to buy that you don't love every last thing about being a vet, *especially* the animals. You got the biggest heart I've ever seen, girl," he said, motioning to a low stone wall. He easily lifted himself up on it and stood on the ledge, scanning the scenery. Then he turned around and extended his hand, wiggling his fingers at her. "Up you go."

She took his hand, and he easily lifted her up his level. As she balanced on the wall, she gasped, looking out over the entire valley spread before her, with the ruins dotting the fields below. A cool sea breeze blew through her hair. "Hey, Boston?"

She turned to him.

He reached over and very gently, pulled a strand of hair that had blown into her face, tucking it behind her ear, and smiled. "*I* see you."

Talk about knocking her absolutely speechless. She shivered, not because she was cold, but because she was next to Mason, and they were standing there in a silence that felt comfortable, and yet meaningful, too.

She averted her eyes and inspected the wide green valley, breathless. "It's beautiful," she whispered.

"Glad you came?"

She nodded, shivering more as he wrapped his arm around her, squeezing gently.

Definitely.

CHAPTER NINE

Even though the situation with the clinic and her house was pretty dire, as Audrey walked to the clinic that Sunday morning, she couldn't help smiling from ear to ear.

Yes, Mason was an ego. Yes, he was probably too attractive for his own good. And yes, she had more important things to think about than whether that little arm-around-the-shoulder had meant something … nevertheless, thoughts of it kept crowding her mind. She replayed that little incident on the stone wall again and again, like a record on repeat, still feeling the rough calluses on his hand as he took hers, the warm pressure of his arm around her. *I see you.*

Not that the rest of the day had gotten much more interesting. No, after that, they'd hiked through the hills a little, and then stopped off for lunch in the city proper. But he hadn't touched her again, and they'd mostly just made small talk. Still, it was pleasant. More than pleasant. She'd gone to sleep last night with a warm, happy feeling bubbling inside her like champagne, wondering if one floor above her, he was thinking about her, too.

Not to mention that he'd volunteered to fix her mold problem, and was now collecting all the materials to do just that.

She smiled bigger, until she passed another expat on the street who looked at her like she was an insane person. She realized that she probably *looked* like an insane person, practically giggling at absolutely nothing. Wiping the smile off her face, she hurried across the street to find another cardboard box. *Oh no. Please, no more strays.*

She was so focused on it that she barely saw the young woman, maybe twenty or so, standing in front of the veterinary's storefront, trying to peer in the windows.

"*Ciao*," Audrey said to the girl as she went to the door and peeked in the giant box. It was full of cans of cat food and had a sign on it that said, *donazioni.* Donations. Eureka.

"*Ciao*," the girl said, smiling.

As Audrey bent over, doing an inventory of the cans and checking their expiration dates, she could feel the girl's eyes on her. She straightened. "*Come posso aiutarla? So soltanto un po' di italiano,* but … sorry." Can I help you? I only speak a bit of Italian …

The girl was model-thin, wearing faded capri jeans and ballet flats, looking effortlessly chic with her stick-straight black hair to her waist and big, horn-rimmed glasses. "That's all right. I speak English," she said, with only a little bit of an accent. "My name is Concetta Busillo. I live on the south side of town and was happy to hear of an actual vet here. I came to see it with my own eyes. Do you work here?"

Audrey nodded. "Yes, but I'm sorry. We're closed to appointments today. Were you looking to adopt?"

"Oh, no," the girl said, a smile widening on her face showing perfectly straight white teeth. "I'm actually a student at the Università di Palermo. I'm in my last year of veterinary school, but taking a break for the semester to make some money so I can go back."

"Oh. That's great. I love fellow animal lovers! What brings you here?"

"I'm from Mussomeli originally," she said, tossing her long hair over her shoulder and pointing across the plaza's fountain. "Born here. This is a good location. Very busy. It's very good that this place is here. Mussomeli has needed a vet for some time."

"Yes, I've heard that a lot."

Concetta nodded. "I hope one day to do start my own practice here in town. But I have many years to go before that."

"Well, if you ever need any tips or help with your studies, I'm happy to offer—"

"Do you know where I can find this Dr. Smart?" she asked, leaning in. "Is he nice? Do you think he needs another tech or intern to help out around the place?"

Audrey stared at her for a moment. She was used to this, since a lot of times, people thought she was much younger than her thirty-two years. Darn freckles. People always thought she was the tech, not the actual vet. "She's pretty nice. Actually, she's—"

"A she?" The girl clapped her hands. "Oh, good. Much easier to work for a woman. You think she needs help?"

"Definitely. Unfortunately, we don't have the funding to pay for another—"

"That's okay. To tell you the truth, I would do it for free. I'm in my last year of clinicals and every other place on this island has declined me. I *need* those hours in order to graduate," she whispered

60

conspiratorially, something Audrey understood. She'd been through that dance, too, ten years ago. "So do you think she'd be interested?"

"Well," Audrey said, finally finding her keys in her purse. "Actually, *I'm*—"

She stopped when she realized something strange. The door to the front of the clinic was open.

She looked at the girl. "Why is this door open?"

Concetta shrugged. "I don't know. It was like that when I got here."

Audrey peered through the window, trying to see if anything was amiss. Everything looked just as she had left it yesterday morning. The laptop she used to make appointments was sitting on the reception desk, the lock didn't show any sign of being tampered with or forced, and none of the windows appeared to be broken.

Then she realized that Concetta was still standing there. "I'm sorry." She patted her chest. "I'm actually the vet, Dr. Smart."

Her jaw dropped. Audrey might as well have told her she was Kim Kardashian. "You are! Oh my. My apologies. I—"

"It's all right. I don't mind at all. You had no way of knowing. Why don't I take your information and I'll be in touch if we need you?"

"Sure!" She reached into her shoulder bag and pulled out a business card with all of her information on it. "Here it is. I've been throwing these all over town trying to find a job to pay my tuition bill, not that it's been doing me much good. But I promise, I want this so bad I would work here for free. Just call!"

Audrey had to admire her spunk. It reminded her, well, of herself, at that age.

When Concetta had left, Audrey turned her attention to the door. She'd left the clinic yesterday morning, excited about the trip to Agrigento with Mason. Had she just spaced and forgotten to lock the door? Or had someone broken in?

Then she remembered Luca. The fifteen-year-old delivery boy for the hardware store was usually responsible and loved the taking the dogs on walks, but she'd only used him a couple times before. Maybe he'd gotten distracted and forgotten to lock up.

Likely. She'd have to remind him when he came by to drop off the spare key. But she couldn't fault him. He was a volunteer, after all.

Pushing open the door and wedging her body between it and the jamb, she lowered her body and tried to pick up the box. But filled with at least a hundred cans of cat food, it wasn't exactly light. She had to resort to propping the door open with her body, dragging the box in,

61

and letting the door slam closed on its own. As she did, her purse fell off her shoulder. She hoisted it back up, her arms aching from the exertion. The box had to weigh at least fifty pounds.

Sweating now as she backed up, dragging the unwieldy package across the linoleum, she nearly tripped over a chair in the reception area. Instead, the arm of the chair poked her square in the butt.

"Ouch!"

She let out a groan, massaged the sore spot, and altered her course, making so much commotion that the animals down the hall began to join in, barking and howling at her arrival.

"One second, one second, I'm getting there!" she called to them as once again, her purse fell from her shoulder. It wasn't much lighter than the box, truthfully, because of Audrey's affinity for packing everything and the kitchen sink into it.

Pulling it off her arm, she sat it atop the box and continued dragging it, her back now aching.

Just then, one of the dogs let out a particularly ear-splitting howl. "All right! I'm coming!" she shouted, as a kink tore up the muscles of her lower back. She stopped for a second to massage it, and when she straightened and looked back down the hall toward the reception area, she saw something odd.

The chair she'd bumped. It wasn't because she'd gone in the wrong direction of the hallway … it was because it was in the wrong place. Someone had put it out a few feet farther from where it usually sat against the wall, and now it was half in the hallway. No wonder she'd run into it.

"Luca, what were you doing? Arranging furniture?" she murmured, leaping over the box and heading that way to move it back into place. Then she remembered having slept in that area two nights ago, which had required rearranging the chairs. Had she done that?

When she got there, her breath hitched, and for a moment, she was sure she was still dreaming.

It was there in the middle of the reception area, so plain as day that she couldn't believe she'd missed it.

An overweight, balding man, lying on his stomach on the tile floor, in the same place where she'd tried to sleep a couple days before.

Slowly, all her breath left her. That guy looked *unnaturally* comfortable, considering how cold and rock-hard that floor was.

She took a few cautious steps toward him, noting the clipboard under his body and the papers scattered about his head. Wait. That shirt looked familiar. White, short-sleeved, with a buffalo-plaid checkerboard pattern. Not exactly the height of fashion. Scuffed shoes, very worn.

Was that the inspector? What was he doing? Maybe he had his ear to the ground, listening for termites or something. "Um, hel—"

She froze when she saw her silver letter opener, sticking out from the space between his shoulder and his ear.

There was a small pool of blood on the tile underneath it.

Audrey screamed, and the animals in the back room joined in, louder than ever.

CHAPTER TEN

Audrey knew this drill.

She sat in her office, sipping from a paper cup one of the officers brought her from the water cooler in the break room, and trying to stop her hands from shaking.

Funny how she'd seen three dead bodies since she arrived here, and this never got any easier. Especially not now that it was right in her place of work. With her own—gasp—letter opener. She was sure opening her mail would never be the same again.

How brutal. And bloody. The other murders hadn't been like this. They *could've* been accidents. But this one just seemed more barbaric. Someone had come inside, somehow, taken the letter opener, and ...

Her stomach roiled at the thought. She looked up at her Puppies of the Year wall calendar, trying to recapture her Zen.

Fat chance.

Instead of cute little puppies, all she saw was poor Vito Cascarelli, surrounded by a halo of his own blood.

Just then, there was a knock at her door. She looked up to see her old buddy, Detective DiNardo. Okay, they weren't exactly buddies, but he'd come to know her well over the last few cases. He had a no-nonsense, hard façade that made him seem like he cared for no one, but she'd seen his squishy, kind center. He was wearing his normal jacket and tie, as buttoned-up as one could imagine. She motioned him in.

He stepped inside and looked around. Was he looking for clues, even now? "Never a dull moment with you, eh?"

She shrugged. Originally, she'd been the suspect of the past murders, but eventually, her name had been cleared, and she and the detective had maintained a bit of a guarded friendship. Especially since she'd seen to his Persian, Luna. "I suppose not. Sit down, Detective. Please."

He complied. "So you lead an exciting life."

"Is *leads an exciting life* a euphemism for *cursed*?" she asked with a smirk. "Because if so, yes. I agree."

He chuckled.

She tossed the cup in the garbage, laced her fingers in front of her, and placed them on the blotter. "So I suppose you're here to ask me questions."

"At this point, I thought you might already know what I was going to ask, so I wouldn't have to."

She yawned and rubbed her eyes. "I'm too tired to think. So just fire away."

"All right. Let's start with this. The victim, according to his identification, appears to be one Vito Cascarelli of the Mundo apartment complex on via Tripoli. Did you know him?"

She nodded. "Well, not well. But he's the city building inspector. He came over a few days ago to inspect my house, and then the day after that, the clinic."

DiNardo scribbled something in his book. "You pass?"

Audrey gritted her teeth. *I bet this means he's going to say I have a motive. Again.* "No, I did not. Thanks for reminding me."

"Yeah? What's wrong with the place?"

"Ha-ha. Everything. You know that. But it was the hole in the floor that failed the house, and black mold that failed the clinic. I'm taking care of it."

"They *both* failed?"

"Yes," she muttered. "Stop rubbing it in."

"Where have you been staying?"

"A friend's," she said. "On via Milano."

"And this friend of yours will provide you with an alibi?"

"Possibly," she said, thinking of how Mason had let her dangle like a worm on a hook before granting her permission to stay at his place. "Eventually."

DiNardo raised an eyebrow.

"I mean, yes. Of course. I was probably with him when … uh, when do they think the murder happened?"

"Looks like sometime last night, as far as we can tell. When was the last time you were here before today?"

"Yesterday morning. I came by to check on the animals, locked up the place, and went to Agrigento for the day. Got back at around nine in the evening, and we were so tired, we went right back to the house and I went to sleep. Then I got in here at around eight, to find the door open and this guy lying dead in my lobby."

"The door wasn't forced. Anyone else have a key?"

She nodded. "Luca ... I don't know his last name. From the hardware store. I gave it to him yesterday because he walks the dogs for me when I'm going to be gone for a while."

DiNardo wrote more. "So you were with a friend all night ... where?"

"His house. Via Milano."

"And you were with him all night?"

Well, that sounded rather tawdry. Not to mention, wrong. "I was in his house. But ..."

"But?"

She shuffled in her seat. But ... was that good enough? He was upstairs, she was down. She could've easily slipped out to murder the guy. Not that she *had*, but she knew enough of the way Detective DiNardo worked to know one thing ...

Her alibi wasn't watertight. Not in the least.

"I wasn't in the same room as him, no. So I'm supposing he's not the best of alibis since I could've left the house without him seeing me. But the thing is, yes, it sounds bad that Vito Cascarelli flunked me, but really, I liked the guy. He was nice. I told him I'd fix everything right up so he could inspect it. I didn't *kill* him."

"Mmmhmm," he said, not looking up.

Oh no, here we go with the mmmhmms again. "I have absolutely no idea what he was doing in here. I'm telling you. Or how he got in. It's just bizarre."

"Well ... one theory is that he came to do another inspection, failed you again, and—"

"And I stabbed him with my letter opener? Really?"

"Oh, so you recognize the weapon?"

She stiffened. Had she incriminated herself? "Yes. Of course I do. It's mine. Actually, it came with the building, but I took it as mine. It usually sits on the reception desk in a little pencil cup." She shrugged. "I recognized it because it's kind of distinctive, with that diamond shape on the top. But anyone there could've taken it and used it."

"Yes, and with a weapon like that, a woman could've done the deed just as easily as a man."

Audrey let out a big puff of air and stared at the detective. "Why don't you just come out with it?"

He pulled on the collar of his starched dress shirt. "What's that?"

"That I'm not allowed to leave the city while you're investigating because I'm a possible suspect. Blah, blah, blah. Right?"

"Bingo. See, Audrey, you could be a detective here. You've practically got it all down."

She sighed. It was nice to have *one* thing down, since the rest of her life was completely up in the air. When he stood up, she did, too. "I really want you to find the person who did this," she told him earnestly. "And not just because it happened here. I'm not putting on a show. Despite what you might think, I liked the man. He was very kind to me. He even told me that I could call him at any time and he'd rush right back to—"

She paused, as light-bulb of inspiration struck her.

"What is it, Dottore Smart?"

"Well, I was just thinking. When he failed me for the black mold, he was beside himself. Very upset, because I could tell he was an animal lover. He told me that the second I got it fixed, he'd come over and reinspect so that I could begin operations right away," she said, tapping her chin in thought. "Maybe someone called him in, pretending to be me?"

The detective nodded. "Could be. Did anyone else know about that deal you made?"

She shook her head. "No. No one …"

Well, except Mason.

But he wouldn't do that. That was crazy. She'd accused him once and been wrong before. She wasn't even going to go down that path.

DiNardo was still waiting for her to continue, but she waved it away. "Never mind. Probably has nothing to do with it."

"All right. Hey," he said, eyes narrowed. "Can you give me the name of the friend you stayed with so I can check it out?"

"Oh. Um, sure, It's Mason Legare. He's at Ventidue via Milano," she said, wondering if he could see right through her, to her innermost thoughts. For some reason, she felt compelled to add, "We're just friends."

He raised an eyebrow. "You said that."

Great, way to make yourself look more suspicious just because you can't handle being an adult with normal adult relationships.

He scribbled more down and said, "All right. Thank you."

"Right. Well," she motioned to hallway. "If we're done here, I have a litter of baby bunnies to see to."

"By all means. Except …"

She cringed and turned, knowing she was not going to like this.

He snapped his fingers for an officer who was hovering in the hallway. "I'm going to have to ask an officer to accompany you. Any time that you're in the building. I don't want you to be in here alone. This is a crime scene, and we need to keep it clean. I'll allow you and only you to come in and take care of the animals, but until we learn more about who did this, I need everyone else to stay away. Do you understand?"

"How long will that take?"

"Couple days. Maybe more."

A couple days felt like a lifetime, considering all the work she had to do. But she bit the bullet. "All right. That's fine. Anyway, I have a black mold problem, and I was planning to have someone come in to—"

"Not until this investigation is complete."

"But the mold can't be good for the animals—"

"From what I read on the report on the door, it's in a different area and should not affect them."

"Yes, *should*. But he didn't know for sure. And if there's any chance their health could be affected, then—"

"Then you'll have to arrange to move them out of here," he said, in a final way that told her not to test him.

She gritted her teeth. He might as well have written *Not to be trusted* in Sharpie on her forehead. After all she'd done for him and Luna? Well, she assumed it was probably just standard procedure, but it made her feel about two inches tall.

"Yes, of course. I understand," she said, as he moved aside, letting her pass through.

When she did, she could feel his eyes on her, boring into her back, and that's when she knew it.

This is wonderful. You're suspect number one again, Audrey. How lucky.

And that meant only one thing. She'd have to find a way to swerve their suspicions in the direction of the real murderer. Whoever that was.

CHAPTER ELEVEN

Things on the life-and-work front just went from bad to worse, Audrey thought as she went back to her House of Horrors to take stock of what supplies she needed to fix the hole in the ceiling.

As she walked, she noticed people were looking at her again. Or was that all in her mind? Every time a new murder cropped up, she always felt like people were blaming her. Now, even more so, because it'd happened right in her reception area.

She shivered at the thought, hugging herself as she walked down the uneven cobblestone street, even though it was quite warm.

Her phone started to ring on the way. She picked it up. It was Brina, who'd been texting her non-stop since the selfie she'd sent from Agrigento the day prior. But Audrey's phone had died on the trip and she hadn't had her charger with her; plus she hadn't had the time to respond.

Now, as she thought of the sight of that poor man, lying dead, she really wished she could curl up in bed with Brina, like they used to as kids. Whenever she'd have a nightmare, instead of running to her parents' bedroom, she'd run to Brina, and Brina would hold her and make everything better, usually by telling some silly, meandering story about two sister princesses that made absolutely no sense.

A phone call from Brina, Audrey decided, was the next best thing. She lifted the phone to her ear to spill all her woes when Brina screamed, *"Abbbbbbbs!"*

Oh, right. Showed where her sister's priorities were.

"Stop, already. You know, Mason thinks you're some crazy lunatic who's obsessed with him."

"Does he?" She seemed proud of the fact. "Well, I'm only obsessed because I want to make him a member of the family."

"Believe me. If he isn't already running for the hills, if you tell him that, he *will* be."

She made a clucking sound with her tongue. "Why didn't you call me last night when you got back? I was waiting!"

"Sorry, I—"

"Doesn't matter. So what happened? Anything juicy?" She was speaking a mile-a-minute, like she couldn't wait for Audrey to spill.

"Not really. I mean, he's sweet. I like him. But ..." She shivered as once again, the image of Vito Cascarelli, lying dead in her reception area, crossed her mind.

"But what? If he's sweet, good with a hammer, and that hot, he sounds like the total package. Is there something I'm missing that the camera didn't reveal? Dandruff? Halitosis? What?"

"No. He's perfect. And I like him. But I have other things on my mind now."

"Oh. So what if the house failed inspection? Invite that hottie to come and help you fix it up, and then the inspector will pass you with flying colors. Meanwhile, the two of you can get coz—"

"The inspector isn't going anywhere," she said as she turned onto the street down which she'd find the *piazza* where she lived. "Since I found him this morning in the lobby of my clinic with a letter opener buried in his throat."

A long pause. "Um. Say that again?"

"Look, I can't talk right now, but I promise I'll call you later, okay?"

"NO! You can *not* end the call on that note!"

"I have to. I'm sorry. I promise I'll call later."

"You'd better," Brina said, as she ended the call.

Audrey stepped to the doorway, and the first thing she noticed was the bright, white sign that hadn't been there the day before, taped at eye-level. *Attenzione!*

It matched the one on the door of the clinic. It had probably been posted there by the inspector, prior to his untimely demise.

As Audrey was throwing open the door, a window across the street popped open. Audrey groaned as a voice said, "Hi, *neighbor*, haven't seen you in a while!"

Audrey turned around reluctantly. "Hi."

"Just wanted to tell you, if you see camera crews around, it's just for little ol' me!" Nessa said with a smile. She appeared ready for her close-up, since Audrey could see her lipstick and fake eyelashes from across the street. "They're starting preliminary work. You know. Studio business."

Audrey didn't really know, and didn't want to know. Before, she'd been a little worried that a camera filming across the street might inadvertently catch her in her bathrobe or something, but those worries had recently been eclipsed by much larger ones. "Gotcha."

"You think you might be able to … I don't know … move that sign until filming's over?" she asked, wrinkling her nose. "It kind of interferes with the charm of the street."

"I don't think I'm allowed to touch it," Audrey replied, trying to scoot through the door.

"I don't think anyone would stop you. So, you failed, hmm? That's a shame. Is that why you killed the inspector?"

Audrey's jaw dropped. *Son of a …* For some reason, Nessa was always the first to know any gossip around this town. Not to mention, the first to accuse Audrey whenever any wrongdoing happened in town. She whirled.

Nessa held her hands up in surrender. "Kidding! I'm just kidding. Although, it does make you a pretty good suspect, doesn't it?"

"Maybe. But I'm not one, since I have an alibi. I was with someone at the time," she said, almost *hoping* Nessa would ask who. "I find it suspicious that you know about it, since it only happened last night."

She shrugged, inspecting her lavender-painted fingernails, and blew on them. "What can I say. I'm a news magnet. It travels straight into my ears, sometimes. I can't even control it. I heard that the body was found in your clinic, is that true?" she called.

Audrey nodded.

"And that it was all mangled and gross?"

"No, it wasn't—"

"But is it true he failed the clinic's inspection, too?"

Oh my God, Audrey thought, staring at her. DiNardo should've gotten her on the force, with everything she knew. "Yes. But I liked him. He was a nice—"

"But that really gives you double the reason to kill him. Did he come by, wanting to put one of those papers on your clinic door, and you offed him, then?"

Audrey frowned. Actually, now that she thought about it, there wasn't a paper on her clinic's front door. Maybe that was what he had gone there for, and somehow, he'd gone in.

"Your silence doesn't make you look any less guilty!" she called. "Trust me!"

"Hmm," Audrey mumbled. She'd had about enough of this conversation, even before it started. "Have a good day."

"You're not going in there?" Nessa shouted in alarm.

71

Audrey stopped with one foot in the door. "It's my house, so yeah. I was planning t—"

"It's a death trap. You can get killed."

"Well, I have to fix whatever is—"

"*Hire* someone. Like I did."

"I don't have the money or the backing of a television studio, unfortunately."

"Still. You do it yourself and the whole ceiling's liable to fall in on you. Don't come crying to me if that happens."

"If that happens, I'll be stuck under a pile of rubble, so I probably won't," she muttered, though Nessa was probably the last person she'd "cry" to. In fact, if it ever happened that Audrey's renovations killed her, Nessa would probably throw a party. And videotape it for one of her episodes. "I'll see you."

She went inside and closed the door, heaving a sigh of relief when she'd finally closed herself off from her pesky neighbor. At that point, she looked up at the roof, and decided it caving in on her would actually be preferable to enduring a conversation with Nessa.

She looked around the house sadly. She'd only left here a few days ago, and now it felt foreign, desolate... nothing like the home she'd hoped to create. She grabbed a pen and paper and started to make a list of supplies to get at the hardware store, but Nessa's words kept coming back to her, again and again.

So that's why you killed the inspector?

Yes, she had a motive. He'd been killed in her clinic. With her letter opener. It made sense that Audrey would be their top suspect.

So now, she'd have to do what she always did. Clear her name so the police could stop focusing on her and catch the real bad guy.

As if she didn't have anything *else* on her plate.

CHAPTER TWELVE

Audrey agreed with Nessa that she probably should've enlisted someone else's help for the massive job of renovating the second-story flooring. And Mason, her number one source of free labor, was the obvious choice.

But he was her alibi, and she'd already been relying on him for shelter. As much as Brina tried to shove them together, that was usually when the floor dropped out from under her. So she decided to try to figure out the renovations on her own.

After all, there's a YouTube do-it-yourself video for everything! she thought as she made her way into the little ma-and-pa hardware store down the street. She had two purposes for the visit; one, to scope out the materials, and two, to talk to Luca, get her key back, and ask him if he'd seen anything.

When she went into hardware stores with her father, there'd always been an air of excitement. The smell of fresh-cut pine boards, fertilizer, and paint mingled together, presenting an air of possibility. She'd become quite an expert on where to find things in the tiny Mussomeli store, even though displays were listed in Italian and there seemed to be very little rhyme or reason to placement. But right then, standing there alone, among the tightly packed aisles, she felt slightly terrified.

This was the biggest job she'd ever taken on, thus far. Part of her wanted to do it herself. Even if her dad wasn't there to see it, she felt like he'd be proud of her for attempting it. He'd said things like that to her before, when she was hesitant about taking on a task, like her first use of the drill, or the first time she punched a nail with a hammer. *You don't know if you can do it unless you try, right?*

Right. And if she screwed up, she could always go crying to Mason for help. That is, if she weren't trapped under the rubble of her mistake.

Not seeing Luca or anyone else among the aisles, she looked down at her list. She needed two-by-fours, probably a lot of them, but she wasn't sure how many. Plywood. More nails for her nail gun. Adhesive. Not to mention, a lot of prayers.

As she started loading the materials onto her cart, she felt the presence of a form standing in the doorway, blocking out some of the afternoon light. She looked up and saw the tall, lanky teen with the thick, every-which-way dark hair. He was dragging in his own cart, likely returning from a delivery.

He stood, silhouetted in the door, fidgeting a bit, looking like he wanted to bolt. When she waved to him, he darted his eyes to the side, like he wanted to make a break for it.

Something was up. That wasn't like him. The boy was a high school heartbreaker, a G-in-training. The first time she'd met him, he'd flirted with her, never mind that she was twice his age.

"Luca? Are you okay?" she called, moving closer.

She had a bit of a history with the boy. He was trustworthy and sweet, and always delivered her stuff on time, which was why she usually tried to tip him well. She walked over to him and was just coming out from the aisle when a tiny dynamo made up of a mess of dark, curly hair, sharp, red-painted fingernails, and perfume rushed up to her. The little Sicilian lady began to scream something at Audrey in rapid-fire staccato Italian. *Guai.* Trouble.

Though her Italian still wasn't the best, Audrey was pretty sure the woman was saying that *Audrey* was the trouble.

This was Luca's mom, and the co-owner of the hardware store with Luca's father.

Though they'd gotten off to a rocky start when she first arrived in Mussomeli, Audrey had hoped that by buying all of her supplies at the store, she'd get into the woman's good graces. Apparently not. The woman was screaming so loud, her face so red, Audrey thought she might have a heart attack. There were only a few people in the store, but now they were all staring at Audrey.

"I'm sorry? I can't speak ... I don't understand ..." she stammered, too shocked to even think of the Italian words for "I don't speak Italian." Besides, the lady had seen Audrey many times before, and during almost all those visits, Audrey had stammered awkwardly though her requests for various materials. The woman knew darn well Audrey had little idea what she was saying.

Luca came over and said some calming words to his mother. They exchanged a few heated sentences, but eventually, the woman quieted down, let out a dramatic sigh, and headed behind the cash register, still giving Audrey the evil eye.

Luca motioned Audrey outside, to the sidewalk. When she got there, Audrey rummaged through her purse for the proper cash to pay the boy for his services. As she did, she said, "Why does your mom hate me now?"

He raked his hands through his dark hair. "It's nothing. She says she thinks you killed the man in your clinic."

Audrey's eyes bulged. "She said that?"

"And she thinks that because you made me go there, you're setting me up to be ... how you say ... the goat?"

She understood. "Scapegoat?"

He nodded. "Yes. That. She thinks the next time the police come, they throw me and you in jail and hide the key."

"Next time? You mean, the police came here already?"

He swallowed. "Yes. Asking me questions. Many, many questions. I tell them I know nothing." He scraped his top teeth over his lower lip. "You think they will?"

"Will what?"

"Throw us in jail? Mama say if she use her savings for jail I no have money for university and have to work as a delivery boy until I die." He shuddered. "I no can do that. Not for her."

"No. No, of course not. Luca, now listen to me. Don't panic. They have no reason to put you in jail at all. You didn't do anything wrong. Neither did I." She looked over at the woman behind the register, who was still shooting eye-daggers as she rang up another customer. "Feel free to tell your mother that. The last thing I need is to be banned from your store. I need you guys for my renovations."

He shrugged, sheepish. "But that's my mama. I don't think you're bad. I like you. I tell her that. She don't listen. She's ..." He waved her away and spun a finger near his ear. "Cuckoo."

"I was as shocked as you were to find out about it," she said, shuddering once again as the thought of poor Vito floated through her brain. "That's why I wanted to come see you. You walked the dogs, right?"

He nodded, reaching into his pocket and pulling out the spare key. "Yes. I tell all this to the police. I was there for about an hour. After dinner. Sun was just going down."

She took the keys and shoved them in her purse. "And nothing was amiss?"

He shrugged. "No. Nothing."

"You didn't see the inspector at all?"

He shook his head. "I saw no one. Even when I walk the dogs. I didn't pass a single person. I just walk them, fill water bowls, clean the litter. Fed the rabbits, like you show me. No problem. Everything normal. No dead body."

She nodded. That meant that the murder must've happened in the night, like DiNardo had said. At that time, she and Mason were on their way back, or at his house. They'd had a couple drinks and talked a little in the kitchen, but they'd both been tired from their explorations, so they went to bed at around ten. Separately, despite what Brina would've liked.

That meant that really … she didn't have much of an alibi. Mason's wonderful couch was just steps from the door. She easily could've slipped out and back in.

Darn it.

"Luca," she said carefully, not wanting to cast any blame on her volunteer, "when I got there this morning, the door was open a bit. It didn't appear to be forced. Did you lock it?"

His eyes widened and he rubbed nervously at the back of his neck. "Er … I … I don't know."

"It's okay if you didn't. I mean, you're not in trouble or anything."

He let out a sigh. "I might have not. I am sorry." He lifted his phone from his pocket. "I got a call as I leave. From *girlfriend*." He whispered the last part, like it was some big conspiracy. "From school. She make me all crazy in the head."

"Oh." Audrey winked, as if she was in on it. "It's all right. I get it. Then you went back home?"

He nodded. "Yes. That's it."

"And you saw no one at all on the way there, or the way back? Anything suspicious at all?"

A wrinkle appeared above his brow as he thought. "No … well …"

"Yes?"

"Well, I did see a black car. Tiny one. It go down the street, very slow. Like it was looking for something. I thought that funny. Usually cars go down that street slow, but not this slow. I could not see in. Windows were dark."

"Oh. Did it stop in front of the clinic?"

"No … it just roll forward, real slow. That's all."

"Okay. Well. Thanks."

He shrugged. "Sorry. I was no help to police either. I think they never find out who kill that man. I bet he had many people who no like him."

That was right. It wasn't just her. Hadn't Vito said that before? He was going hard on a lot of people at the urging of his supervisors. A lot of people were angry at him. Sure, he'd been found in *her* clinic, but that meant absolutely nothing. After all, if she really wanted to murder him, she could think of about a million places to do it that would be better than her own clinic.

"I think they will," she said, stepping back toward the double doors to the hardware store. She wasn't sure she wanted to go back in there and subject herself to the torture that was Luca's mom.

Besides, she had an idea. An itch. A hankering for the truth.

Whenever an injustice like this presented itself to her, she couldn't simply sit by and do nothing. She had to act, even if it got her in trouble. And there were plenty of people who had reason not to like Vito Cascarelli. She just had to find the right one.

I'm sure they will find the killer, she thought to herself. *Because I'm the one who's going to make it happen.*

CHAPTER THIRTEEN

"Dead?"

Audrey sighed. "Yeah. He's dead. The inspector you were so fond of speaking ill of. He was found lying dead, stabbed, in my reception area."

Mason usually didn't show surprise, but his mouth dropped open. "Heck. Really? I was just heading over there with my supplies to—"

"Well, forget that. It's a crime scene. They're only letting me in to care for the animals. I don't know when it's going to open now."

He crossed his arms and stooped a little to look in her eyes. She averted them. "You're all shook up about this."

"Duh. Of course I am. I found a dead man in my place of work. I think I deserve to be a little freaked out."

"All right. So what are you doing?"

She couldn't tell him what she had in mind—that she wanted to snoop. He was firmly against her doing that, since she'd stuck her head in the lion's jaws plenty of times before, only to almost get it snapped off. "I don't know. I have to go back to the clinic."

"You want company? You know, because of ..."

Because of the dead man that was found there? She shuddered again, but shook her head adamantly. "I'll be fine."

"You sure? You look rattled. Come on. Why don't you forget the clinic right now? I'll buy you lunch. I'll let you pick the place, as long as it isn't that—"

"No," she said, more forcefully than she'd have liked. His face fell. He was probably catching onto the fact that she didn't want him with her, no matter what she did, so she decided to soften the blow. "Raincheck? I really do have to get back to the clinic to check on those bunnies."

He shrugged. "Whatever you say."

It was only when she got outside that she heaved a sigh of relief. She peered up at his house, at the windows, feeling bad about lying. But right now, she wanted answers.

Needed them.

It wasn't hard to find the homes of other people who'd had their Certificates of Occupancy revoked, thanks to the glaring white paper on their doors. When Mason had mentioned a couple of his buddies had gotten the same treatment she had, he'd motioned up the street, so she had a pretty good idea of where to go.

She stopped at the first house, a red-painted, impossibly narrow home, sandwiched between two others. It had pretty shutters with starburst cutouts on them, and was actually kind of charming, in a woodsman's cottage kind of way. There were cans of paint lined up at the front door, and there was a ten-speed bicycle hooked over one of the railings. As far as Audrey could see, the only thing wrong with it was the *Attenzione!* notice on the front door.

Checking down the street to make sure Mason wasn't following her, she crept closer to the notice. Sure enough, there was a name written on it: Roberto Gonzales. Underneath, someone had scribbled something in Italian: *Se stai cercando Roberto, sta Hotel Paladino, via Maria.*

Audrey quickly plugged that into her trusty translation app on her phone, already having a good idea of what it said: *If you're looking for Roberto, he's at the Hotel Paladino on via Maria.*

Which, luckily, wasn't too far from the clinic. She passed it every day on her way over there.

And, even better, it was out of sight of Mason's possibly prying eyes.

Not that she didn't want him to know what she was up to. Okay, well, she didn't. If the last few scrapes she'd gotten into were any indication, if she told him she was poking around, she knew exactly what he'd do. He'd try to talk her out of it, tell her it was too dangerous.

But talking to a couple of his friends wouldn't be dangerous. It was fine. *Perfect*, she thought.

The hotel was a nondescript little building that looked like one of the many abandoned properties surrounding it. The only difference was that instead of having a sign on the door announcing that it was available to buy, this sign said *Hotel Paladino.* The sign was wedged against the only window in the place, behind a cage of metal bars that gave it an overall "prison" ambience. When she pulled the door, a smell like burnt popcorn mixed with cigarette smoke and garbage wafted out.

Gathering her courage, she walked across the cramped room, which had dark-paneled walls and was full of mismatched furniture in bright rust and avocado colors, likely from fifty years ago. There was a coffee table scattered with old newspapers, and an ashtray full of cigarette butts.

Holding her breath as she crossed to the reception, she was about to ring the service bell when a woman with bright burgundy hair, who was hiding behind the desk reading a magazine, muttered an unenthusiastic, *"Ciao."*

She said something else, still not looking up from her reading material, but Audrey didn't understand. "No, I don't want a room," she said. "I wondered if you could tell me if you have a guest named Roberto Gonzales?"

The woman looked at her, a confused expression on her face. She'd looked younger at first glance, but now, the lighting was so bad that Audrey could see the woman's heavy cake-makeup, seeping into every little line and crack on her face. Her eyes lit up, and when she smiled, Audrey saw lipstick on her teeth. "Roberto? Ah, Roberto!"

She ripped a little Post-it off a pad and scribbled something on it, then handed it over. It said 2B. The woman pointed through doors to a dark narrow stairwell that looked a little frightening, like a stairway to hell. "Thank you."

Audrey made it to the door without much trouble, except the stench seemed to get worse now, with the addition of something close to cat urine. At 2B, she knocked.

At first, no one answered, so she knocked again. And one more time. Just as she was about to leave, a voice started shouting through the door in Italian. She weakly translated it to, "I don't need housekeeping!"

She knocked again. "Roberto? I'm not housekeeping. I'm Audrey Smart. I wanted to talk to you."

The door opened a crack, revealing a dark-skinned man with a shaved head and bushy beard. His bloodshot eyes, which suggested he'd had a rough night, scanned her from head to toe. "Audrey?" he said with a bit of an accent she couldn't place.

She nodded.

"You American?"

She nodded again.

His eyes narrowed. "What do you want to talk to me about?"

Definitely Latino. "I saw that you had your CO revoked by the inspector. Mine was revoked, too. I was wondering if I could ask you a few questions about it."

A male voice behind him said something. He looked back into his apartment and muttered, "Some woman. She wants to ask me questions about the inspector." He looked back at her. "We both did, me and Dom."

"Oh. You're both here? Can I talk to you?"

He shrugged, then threw open the door as an invitation. The room was about the size of a closet, with no windows, and a stuffy, overwhelming wall of heat hit her. Any invitation she got from his gesture was one to stay away. For a moment, the impulse to flee almost overwhelmed her, but once she took the first step forward, she was able to take another.

As Rob trailed back to a lumpy mattress and threw himself down on it, she realized he was only wearing a pair of tighty-whities. Averting her eyes, she landed on Dom, a tall blond guy who was at least in the process of throwing an old T-shirt over his skinny, pimpled chest.

Dom at least had some manners, because he extended his hand. "Hey. I'm Dom. From New Zealand."

"Hi. Audrey Smart. Nice to meet you. You said your place wasn't up to passing, too?"

He nodded. "Busted sewer line. Thought the city should take care of it. Apparently not."

He motioned to a harvest yellow pleather chair, which was the only furniture in the room, aside from two small twin beds and a night table that was covered with take-out cartons and a couple of empty bottles of liquor. The chair had someone's permanent backside-print on it. There were two pieces of artwork on the wall: one, a small wooden cross, which was hung in such a way that it seemed crooked, and just under it, a print of Davinci's *The Last Supper*.

Audrey preferred to stand.

"So what's this all about? You think we can get a group of us together and try to fight it?" Dom said, sitting on the edge of the bed. "It won't work. I camped out at city hall. They told me the only way I was going to pass was by fixing the problem. I told them, it's *their* problem. It has to do with the sewer line running into the house. But they got stuffing in their ears. They don't listen."

She said, "Actually, no. It's about the inspector. Vito Cascarelli?"

Roberto rolled over in bed, scratched his armpit, and reached for his cigarettes and a lighter. He poked one in his hairy mouth and started to light up. "What about him?"

"He's dead."

The cigarette Roberto was lighting fell from his mouth, and he almost lit his beard on fire. "No kidding."

"Murdered."

The two men exchanged looks. "I don't believe it. Murdered?" Dom asked, as Roberto realized he'd lost his cigarette and pawed around the pile of sheets for it.

She nodded, proud to have had the desired effect of knocking an entire room silent. "In my clinic. Someone stabbed him."

Dom ran a hand through his long, shaggy hair, his mouth an exaggerated O. "Wow. So what are you here for?"

"I was just wondering where you two were last night?" she asked, trying to sound innocent. But really, there was no way to make *I want to know if you killed this guy* sound innocent.

The corner of Dom's mouth quirked up. "You think one of us did it because we held a grudge against the man? Is that it?"

"No. I'm just trying to piece things together. It happened at my business last night, so naturally the police are coming to me. I'm assuming from the shock on your faces that the police haven't interviewed you."

They both shook their heads.

Great. Two perfectly credible suspects, and the cops were dragging their heels on it again. Of course, there could be dozens of people on the list of homeowners who failed inspection. Maybe hundreds. Maybe the police just hadn't gotten to them yet.

"Look," Roberto said, finally succeeding in lighting that cigarette. "Last night, we were at a bar called Costello's on the north side until closing, which was about three. We have about twenty people who were there with us and can verify that. Then we stumbled home together and went to bed. The lady downstairs probably has it on the video camera in the lobby. That's it."

She nodded. "Thanks. Well, you'll probably have to tell the police the same thing in a bit." *If they do their job right.*

Roberto let out a large cloud of smoke and started pushing stuff on the table aside before picking up his ashtray and setting it in front of him on the bed. "Thanks for the warning."

Audrey hated cigarette smoke, but she was curious. "So did you guys know each other before this?"

Dom shook his head. "Nope. Just met here two months ago and are already best mates."

"That's nice," she said. She thought about asking them about Mason, but her eyes were watering from the stench, so she decided to make her exit. "All right, well—"

But before she could thank them and get away, Dom said, "What's wrong with your place?"

"Oh. I have a hole in the ceiling. You have a sewer issue?"

He nodded and motioned to his friend. "Rob's got a little of everything."

Rob looked at the ceiling. "Don't remind me."

She smiled. "And I thought I'd bought the worst property in Mussomeli."

Rob sighed. "I call my place the Little Red Hell. Something has gone wrong with it every day. I'm handy, but at this point, I think the place is laughing at me."

"Are you trying to fix it?" She coughed.

He nodded and flicked the ashes off his cigarette, into the ashtray. "Eventually, when I get the money. Hey—maybe the next inspector will be a woman and we can charm her into passing us?"

He actually posed that question to Dom, who nodded as if it was a great plan. Audrey rolled her eyes. No wonder Mason hung out with these dudes. They all thought they were so smooth with the ladies. But Audrey'd seen more charm in a field of donkeys.

"Well, thanks, again," she said, feeling like she'd hit a dead end. "Hey. Do you know of anyone else who failed their inspection?"

Roberto shook his head, but Dom said, "Yeah. Actually. There was a guy we met. Big guy, looked like Arnold. Kind of angry. German. Uh …" He looked over at Rob. "Remember? At the bar? He left early, too."

Roberto nodded. "Right! Yeah, what was he so angry about?"

"His renovation, on via Camilla. He'd just failed. Remember? What was his name? Hans?"

"Horst."

"Right. Horst. That's it."

Audrey smiled. An angry guy who'd left early that night and had also just failed his inspection? That looked good. Very good. "You said he's on Camilla?" she asked, backing toward the door. She'd already begun choking on the cigarette smoke and was probably only seconds away from hyperventilating. As they nodded, she opened the door. "Thanks, guys. Good luck with your renovations."

She escaped out into the hallway, taking deep breaths of air before remembering this air was almost as foul. She hurried outside and finally took her first breath of clean air. The bright sun was shocking compared to the enclosed, dark dreariness of inside that hotel. Wiping the tears from her eyes, she smiled.

No, she didn't have answers, but she'd done what she needed to do. And now she had a new lead. That was probably the best she could hope for.

CHAPTER FOURTEEN

Because it was on the way, Audrey decided to check in on the animals at the clinic. When she got there and saw the yellow crime scene tape, she remembered she had to text DiNardo before she could go in.

The officer came right away, but even with him there watching her, it was still eerie. She did her best to ignore that spot in reception, speeding through her chores. It wasn't an easy time, having to take care of pets mere steps from where a man had lost his life. Her clinic was cute, reflecting her personality, with the bright white walls and the photographs of baby animals everywhere, but if anything could turn it into a house of horrors, that was it. She was constantly looking over her shoulder as she gave the little bunnies their bottles.

Luckily, though, they were so adorable, and appeared to be growing under her care. It was hard to think of evil when cuddling a tiny little bunny that wouldn't even fill a teacup.

When she finished up, she burst outside as if the black mold and the ghost of Vito Cascarelli were chasing her. Then she thanked the officer, and they parted ways.

It was about three as she used her phone to guide her to via Camilla. After having missed lunch due to her eagerness to get away from Mason, she was starving, so she stopped at a little street vendor on the way and got something called a *Scaccia*, which was kind of like a cross between lasagna and a calzone. As she was nibbling the crust and trying not to let the grease from the pepperoni dribble down her chin, she turned onto via Camilla and immediately heard the construction racket, halfway down the street.

There was a pretty home there with a massive balcony and a rustic, arched doorway, behind construction scaffolding. Audrey spied the sign from the inspector on the door as she approached. When a large, intimidating man with gray, buzzed hair walked out, grunting, she knew she'd found the right place.

"Hello," she called as he dumped a bucket of brown water on the ground. "Mr. ... um. Are you Horst?"

He turned to her, frown deepening. "What if I am?"

85

"I'm Audrey Smart. I just—"

"Are you the new inspector?" he said in a thick German accent. "As you can see, renovations are ongoing. Come back later."

So he knows something happened to the inspector, she thought, adding that to the growing list of suspicions she was compiling in her head. "I'm not the inspector. I'm another person whose house the inspector flunked, and I wanted to ask you some questions."

He started to walk away, disinterested, then seemed to think better of it, because he stopped. "No time."

"It'll only take a second." She followed him, still clutching her half-eaten sandwich. "Anyway, what's wrong with your house?"

She almost made it to the doorway when he turned on her, so quickly and unexpectedly, she nearly poked him in the breastbone with her nose. The guy was huge. Huge and scary. Despite being older than most of the regular one-euro people, probably pushing seventy, he didn't look any less intimidating. "Plumbing issue, electrical ... it's BS."

"I understand. You have experience renovating houses?"

"Me? I have the most experience! I remodel houses all over Germany. Big ones, small ones. For over fifty years! My father was a contractor. My father's father was. I learned from the best. And this man comes in and fails *me*?" He huffed, his face reddening, the creases on his forehead deepening. "It's... *unglaublich!*"

He looked a little like he was about to blow a gasket, and Audrey didn't want to bother him anymore, so she took a step back.

When she did, he pointed at her chin. "You have ..."

She wiped at it and found a huge string of mozzarella had stuck to her face. "Oh. Thanks." Okay, so maybe he wasn't about to kill her. "Your house does look lovely. I'm sorry that happened. You clearly know what you're doing."

"You bet *der hintern* I do."

"I failed three days ago. When did you get the notice that your inspection failed?"

He thought for a moment. "About then, too."

"Yeah, it's funny! That's how I found out that there were a bunch of other people who failed," she went on lightly, trying to be as delicate as possible. "I was talking to my friend who was at the bar with you last night, and they mentioned you'd failed and were unhappy about it. Huh?"

He nodded, but was already eyeing her suspiciously. *Okay, Aud. Be cool or he'll probably pick you up and throw you into the next street over.*

"Had to unwind, right? Have a couple beers, relax … I mean, I personally had a few glasses of wine. It was so stressful."

He continued staring her down, like, *And what's your point?*

"I bet you wanted to just find that guy and …" She shook her fists in front of her, miming someone shaking a person by the shoulders. "Gah! Am I right?"

He frowned. "I only had one beer. I got a call from a lady friend. She was arriving from overseas in Palermo last night, and needed me to pick her up."

"Lady friend?"

"*Ja* … now, what are all these questions for?"

She sighed. She supposed those things could be easily verified, if she asked for the name and the flight, all those things that'd just make him more suspicious of her. So she decided to come clean. "I'm sorry. But the guy was found dead in my clinic and now the police probably think I did it. So I just wanted to see if I could help them in any way."

"Your clinic?"

"Yes. I'm a vet."

He took a deep breath and stepped out again, then sat himself down on the small stone wall outside the house, wiping the sweat from his forehead with the back of his hand. He actually patted the spot next to him for her to sit.

For a second, she thought of her father, holding that postcard out to her and smiling. He was a little gruff, too. He'd left when he was in his mid-forties, but whenever she thought of him, it was as if he hadn't aged a day. Maybe he looked a little like old Horst here.

She scooted next to him and sat as he said, "Don't tell me you want help on your place."

She shook her head. "I'm good. I'll get it done. There's a hole in the second floor, so I'm probably going to have to replace the whole thing."

"A hole?" He tilted his head. "Just patch it. Quick fix."

"Oh, I tried. I put a plank over it, so I wouldn't fall in, but now it really needs to—"

"Still. You patch. It's quick. Nothing like this mess they've got me doing." He jerked a thumb behind him. "Maybe the new inspector will be better."

87

"So you heard that he died. Who told you?"

"The police."

"Oh. They've interviewed you?"

He nodded. That was good; at least they were doing *something*. "Was not something that surprised me. He made enemies all over town, only one month on the job!"

"One month? Really?"

Horst nodded. "Yes. The old inspector, the one before this guy, looked at my place a month ago. He was good. He checked it out. Said all okay. No problems with electric. And then he left, and I got Cascarelli, that *Dummkopf*. Gave me six citations. *Six!*"

It didn't seem right, talking ill about the poor guy for just doing his job. At least, Audrey *assumed* it was ill. She wasn't really sure what a *Dummkopf* was, but it sounded bad. "Well, he told me the city was coming down hard on them to keep to code, to avoid liability issues."

He grunted. "Yeah. Probably fired the other man. The *reasonable* man, in order to give the job to him."

Audrey let that sink in. Yes, that made sense. What if the prior employee was bitter over losing his job and having it go to someone else? That was a possibility. One thing was sure; Vito had a lot of possible enemies. Poor guy.

"Do you know the name of that other inspector?"

He scratched the side of his temple. "Dellisanti. That was it."

"Great. Thanks. I appreciate that." She stood up. If Dellisanti had been fired and replaced, maybe that was a motive for murder, too. It was another lead, at least.

"Audrey, I wouldn't go looking for too much trouble, if I were you," he said.

"Oh, I won't," she murmured, but she was already making plans to track down this disgruntled former inspector, Dellisanti. *And anyway, I don't have to. It usually finds me first.*

CHAPTER FIFTEEN

As Audrey walked back up toward city hall, she passed the same food cart. This time, it was nearing dinnertime, but she couldn't help but get a pistachio granita. It was calling to her.

Despite her poor mood, the center of town was alive and vibrant as usual. When she'd first arrived here, it was much less crowded than it was now. There were people around, shopping at the local stores or getting in their daily exercise, and a couple of girls were playing hopscotch on the sidewalk. The windows of all the homes were open to let in the cool Mediterranean breeze, and the sun was as bright as ever.

She was just maneuvering around them on street, breaking up the chunks of ice with the long spoon, when she saw the elusive Councilman Falco, heading up the steps to the stately building, briefcase in hand.

Rushing to catch up to him, she called, "Councilman!" just as she dropped the thing on the ground. Green ice went sloshing everywhere.

He stopped and went over to her. The man was kind and sympathetic, but also inordinately busy. She always felt like she needed to talk in double-time whenever she was around him. "Uh-oh. Looks like you had an accident."

She sighed. "It's just par for the course with the way my week is going."

His face turned grave. "Yes, I heard about the murder in your clinic."

"I'm sure the whole town has by now. And I'm sure you heard the clinic was closed down by that inspector. Now I can't even make repairs until the police give me the all-clear. I'm allowed to keep strays there until the mold problem is cleaned up but I can't see appointments. So it's a bit of a problem."

She hoped he'd say, *No! I'm shocked! We need to fix that right away. You can't stay closed.* But he simply said, "It's a shame. Certainly. But you get that mold taken care of, and we'll get the new inspector to pass you right away." He patted her shoulder and started to hurry away.

Did he hear anything she'd just said? "Like I said, I can't, until the police—"

"Well, I'm sure they're working as hard as they can."

Audrey was less certain about that. Sure, DiNardo had solved the last two crimes, but if it weren't for her, he'd probably still be searching for clues on the first one.

"Who is the new inspector?" she asked, jogging to keep up with him. "Do you know?"

"No. I don't. I'm not even sure if they've appointed one. But come on in. I'm sure you can ask around inside."

He moved so quickly, she was out of breath by the time she reached the top of the steps. When she got there, he powered inside, almost as if he were *trying* to leave her behind.

"There's the information desk," he said to her, patting her on the shoulder again. "You have any problems, you just see me."

And then, before she could even thank him, he disappeared, almost as if in a puff of air, like a magician. That was the hilarious thing about Falco. He'd been her biggest champion, wanting to get this clinic off the ground, but the second a problem appeared? Poof.

And unfortunately, she seemed to be a problem magnet.

She went over to the lady at the information desk and smiled at her behind the plexiglass divider. "Hi, do you speak English?"

The older woman peered at her over her bifocals. "Yes. What can I help you with?"

"I'm wondering if you know anything about who the new city building inspector i—"

"Building Inspector's Office, Room 134," she said briskly.

"Oh. Okay. Would you be able to tell me the name of the former building—"

"Building Inspector's Office, Room 134," she repeated, almost as if she were a recording.

Well, that was that. Audrey backed away. "Thanks," she said, heading down the long hallway.

She got about halfway down it when she came to the room. Unlike the other doors in the hallway, that one was closed. She knocked, and no one answered. She knocked louder, and for a few more seconds, and there was no response. Pulled the knob. It was locked.

"Thanks a lot, Information Lady," she said, looking around helplessly. It was almost dinner, so maybe he'd gone home for the day.

Audrey noticed a woman in a suit hurrying down the corridor, carrying a stack of papers.

"Excuse me," she said to the woman, feeling a little guilty because this woman seemed even busier than Falco. The woman turned around. "Do you speak English?"

She nodded.

"I was looking for whoever the new inspector is?"

She started to whirl around. "I don't know the hours for that office but I just saw Signore Tomas Dellisanti over that way. He used to work there. You could probably ask him." She pointed behind Audrey. "Last room on the right. Tall. Dark hair. You can't miss him."

"Oh! Great!"

Audrey jumped into action and sped down the hallway, following the woman's directions. When she got there, she pulled open the door, expecting she'd see a waiting room full of people, and would have a hard time picking Dellisanti out. But as she barreled in there, too late, she realized that Dellisanti was in there, standing in front of a large, dark-wood desk, meeting with only one person, a man with a rather square-shaped Marlon Brando head full of white hair.

The two of them turned and stared at her, waiting for an explanation.

She let out a breath.

It was only then that she caught the crest on the outside of the door, and the words *Sindaco Roberto Fanelli*. She wasn't really sure what *sindaco* meant, but clearly, the man behind the desk was an important one.

"Um. Sorry. Wrong room."

She backed herself out and let the door close behind her. It did, but not all the way. It was open a crack, and the man behind the desk was speaking rather loudly. She grabbed her phone and started working her thumbs, trying to translate as fast as she could. *Sindaco* was the first word she put in. It meant "mayor."

Perfect, so she'd crashed a private meeting with the mayor.

Shaking off the embarrassment, she listened and thumbed in more words from the conversation. At first he seemed angry. He pounded the desk with his fist and said something about Cascarelli ruining their revitalization efforts.

Really? Audrey thought. *That poor man was working his tail off to please you guys, and this is how you treat him? Nice.*

91

Whatever it was, Mayor Fanelli was clearly pissed off about it. He kept pounding the desk, as Dellisanti interjected something about how he was in complete agreement. Something about how now he doesn't have to worry, because Cascarelli is gone.

Oh, so Cascarelli was an obstacle? The question was, how ambitious was the mayor? Ambitious enough to remove obstacles, at any cost?

Was it possible the mayor and Dellisanti had something to do with this?

Before that thought could spiral into even more sinister ones, his tone shifted to one that was distinctly more cheerful. Something about offering him the job, having him back. Dellisanti responded enthusiastically with a yes, and they shared a laugh over something Audrey couldn't hear.

Ha-ha. So funny. You kill the guy who took your job and now everything's going your way, isn't it?

She stood there, listening for a while, trying to translate, but her thumbs started to ache. But as she did some thumb gymnastics, trying to stretch them, she realized that she could make out a lot of what they were saying. Really, all they were doing was talking about football and vacation spots and stuff, shooting the breeze. It only fired Audrey up more. A man was dead, a man who'd devoted his life to the city, and they were talking about the best way to see Greece?

By the time they said their goodbyes, Audrey was good and angry.

Audrey just had to put a wrench in whatever plans they were scheming. She almost felt like Vito was nudging her from the beyond, urging her onward. *Give that guy a hard time.*

Audrey pressed her back against the wall as the door opened, but she needn't have worried about him seeing her. He sauntered out like he was all that, his face buried in his phone, which he was holding and scrolling through with one hand. He was nothing like Vito, tall and slim, well-dressed, a man who meant to go places in this world.

As he headed toward the exit, Audrey rushed up behind him.

"Mr. Dellisanti!" she called.

The man turned around, and his confusion morphed into deeper confusion, as in, *Aren't you the lady who stormed my meeting with the mayor?*

"So are you the new inspector?"

The man smiled. "Yes … as of a few moments ago, I am. And who are you?"

"I'm Audrey Smart. I'm—"

"American, eh?"

"Yes. The dead man was found in my veterinary clinic. It's very convenient that Mr. Cascarelli's dead. That means that you get your job back, huh?"

His eyes narrowed and he pulled on the collar of his dress shirt. "Wait … what are you … are you insinuating something? Are you accusing me of killing Vito to get my old job back?"

She shrugged. "If the shoe fits …"

"In this case, you're wrong. Vito was a good friend of mine. We got along well, grew up together. I was very distressed to hear of his passing and I want to get to the bottom of it."

Right. He could just be saying that. "Maybe you were very competitive."

"We weren't." He scoffed. "There was no reason to be. Look. I didn't get fired from the inspector's office in the first place. I was promoted to a nice, cushy desk job. I actually recommended Vito for the inspector job, and he got it. But Mayor Fanelli offered me the inspector job back, at a bit of a pay cut, but what can I do? I took it. Because the work has to get done."

"Oh," Audrey said, feeling foolish. "That's great that it all worked out," she murmured. "I'm sorry. I'm a little on edge because I found the body this morning."

"You found the body?" he repeated, his face turning sympathetic. "I'm sorry. That must've been hard for you."

"Thanks, it's—"

"It's really hard to believe Vito's dead. Our families were tight," he said with a sigh. "Really tight. We did everything together. When I heard—"

He stopped speaking and looked away, trying to collect himself. For a moment, Audrey thought she saw tears in his eyes.

"All I could think was, his poor wife."

"He had a wife?"

He nodded. "Lisa. She's a lovely woman. An artist. Our wives were best friends, years ago. Before they moved to Sutera. I believe that recently, they were having their troubles, going through a divorce. But she loved him very much. She must be devastated."

"Oh. I didn't know." Now she felt worse than ever for the poor man. He had family. Friends. People who cared about him. Including Tomas Dellisanti.

93

No, he wasn't the killer either.

And that meant she was at another dead end.

But maybe there was someone in his personal life who could shed some light on the man that he was. Someone who could lead her closer to the killer. Lisa Cascarelli, from Sutera.

CHAPTER SIXTEEN

It was too late to go all over the place, looking for the ex-wife. Audrey could've gone back to her house and tried to figure out how to fix her floor, but by then, she was too exhausted to think of even doing that. When she returned to Mason's house, she found a tarp there. She lifted it up and found what looked like a bunch of cleaning supplies.

She smiled. He'd bought these to help fix up her clinic? How sweet.

She stood outside the door, wondering if she should knock; after all, she lived there, if only temporarily. She decided she should, just to be on the safe side. She rapped lightly. Then harder.

No answer.

She tried the knob. It was locked.

And she didn't have a key.

Wonderful.

A chittering noise caught her attention. It was Nick. He jumped up on the railing and peered down at her.

"Do you know where he is?"

Nick simply licked his paws.

She slumped down on the front stoop with Nick at her feet, and searched up and down the street, wondering where her lovely host had gone, and how long he'd be. After all the excitement of today, she was bone tired. So much for curling up on the sofa with a glass of wine. She also could've really gone for one of his nice, delicious Southern meals. But she guessed she was out of luck.

Tapping her feet on the stone walk, she found herself getting antsy. It was like there was so much to do, but she was being held immobile.

But no, there were some things she could still do, even here.

She pulled out her phone. She hadn't looked at it in a while, but she had at least twelve messages from her sister, both voicemail and increasingly frantic texts, wanting the scoop on the murder. She'd have to call her back later.

"Okay, Mr. Vito Cascarelli. Let's see if I can find out anything about you and this lovely wife of yours," she murmured, typing his name into the search bar.

95

The search results didn't show much. There were a few websites in Italian that she couldn't read, and he was listed on the city of Mussomeli's website as an employee. She searched more and found a website which listed his address, in north Mussomeli.

There was also an address listed in Sutera, which turned out to be a small town located south. She vaguely remembered passing it on the way to Agrigento. She clicked on the link and noticed that the deed to the property belonged to a Vito and Lisa Cascarelli.

Bingo.

"I wonder if she moved back to Mussomeli, too," Audrey murmured. If so, maybe she had something to do with the murder. Maybe she could question her.

She looked up the name, "Lisa Cascarelli Sutera" and found a website for "Lisa Cascarelli Designs." She clicked on it and scrolled through pictures of brightly colored pottery, to the bottom. It looked like the art studio itself, a small place with plenty of color and artistic flair, was still located in Sutera.

Then Audrey clicked on the "news" section of the website, to find an article about the opening of the pottery business, from only a few months ago. In it was a picture of an older woman, holding one of her creations. She had curly dark hair and a broad smile. Audrey scanned the article, trying to make out the words in Italian, and was proud of herself that she didn't have to use her Google Translate once. It said:

"Lisa Cascarelli has opened up a new pottery business in the heart of Sutera. After ten years of marriage and living as a housewife, a recent bitter divorce left her unsure of her next adventure. The opening of Lisa Cascarelli Designs, she says, has been a healing experience for her, allowing her to do what she loves while bringing beauty and joy to the Sutera area."

Bitter divorce? That sounded promising.

Maybe they weren't quite as in love as Tomas Dellisanti remembered. It was a possibility …

But also, a problem. The widow still lived in Sutera, and Audrey was under firm orders from the police not to leave the city. That meant no going after her, asking questions. She'd done that once before, when trying to get answers about another murder, and it was like the police had a radar for her. The second she even attempted to cross over the border, they'd lunged at her.

It was a good thing she'd gotten to go to Agrigento when she had. If not, maybe she'd really feel trapped.

She found herself thinking of Mason, holding her on that stone wall and smiling down at her, and warmth spread over her chest.

She realized she was grinning goofily when her phone started to ring in her lap.

It was G. She stared at it for a moment. She hadn't spoken to him since the night of the taste-testing. So much had happened since then. "Hello?"

"*Principessa!*" he called. "How are you?"

"Hi, G. I'm fine."

"I've been missing you. It has been a while. Are you doing well?"

"Yes. Very well. But it's only been a couple days!" She felt guilty now, for the way she'd run out on him. For the way she'd misinterpreted his invitation and assumed he wanted more, then got angry at him when she realized his true intentions. It wasn't his fault, and she'd been kind of short with him. She said, "I wanted to apologize for leaving you so abruptly last t—"

"No. Not at all. You were lovely, as always. But you have much on your mind, eh?"

She sighed. "You heard about the inspector."

"*Si.*" That wasn't hard to believe. Everyone in town had by now, and G knew just about everyone. She'd have been more surprised if he didn't know. "In the clinic, yes?"

"Yes. I found the body."

He tutted. "I came by to see you at your home today, but you were gone, *Principessa*. There was a notice on your door. Were you forced out?"

Her shoulders slumped. "Don't remind me. It's been a little bit of a whirlwind since I last saw you, that's for sure."

There was a pause. "*Principessa*. I'm not working dinner tonight. Let's say you and I go for a walk? I can pick you up in five minutes?"

She smiled. She really did need someone to talk to about all this. "How about dinner? I'm starving."

"Dinner it is. I know a place on the edge of town. Very quiet."

Very romantic. The words drifted through her head, but she stamped them down. She'd been through that rodeo before. No need to get her hopes up again. Besides, she wasn't sure, after everything with Mason, she wanted things to go in that direction. "All right. But actually, I'm not at my house, for obvious reasons. I'll come find you. Are you at the café?"

"I am. I'll see you soon?"

She ended the call and looked across the street at the empty lot. The place across from Mason's had once been a row home, but now it was nothing more than a burned-out shell. That was probably better than Nessa's prying eyes and accusing tongue.

"Come on, fox," she said to Nick, jumping to her feet and rushing down the street. The last thing she needed now was for Mason to catch her while on the way to go out to dinner with G.

Not that it was anything more than dinner. Completely innocent. Or…

No. She refused to think about that. Maybe G could help her sort out some of this murder stuff, and give her some ideas on where to go next to get out of this mess. Right now, that was what she needed most.

CHAPTER SEVENTEEN

"*Principessa!*" G shouted when she was still several buildings away from her. He rushed up to meet her, put two hands on her shoulders, and kissed each cheek warmly. "You look beautiful!"

Audrey looked down at herself. She was wearing a T-shirt and jeans, what she'd been wearing the whole day, and her hair was a mess. She felt like she smelled from taking care of the animals and traipsing over creation, trying to get clues to this murder. She surely didn't feel beautiful.

But G was eyeing her in the same way he had when she'd put effort in and worn that flouncy little number to the dessert taste-testing. Either he was pulling her leg, or he was blind.

And G? For the first time, she'd barely recognized him. He wasn't wearing his normal skull cap and white apron over jeans and a white T-shirt. He was wearing a khakis and a nice button-down shirt, and instead of his delicious creations, he smelled of aftershave. Had he dressed up for her?

"Thanks." She yawned. "Sorry I'm not better prepared for dinner. I've had a busy day. I can't wait to sit down and relax. I'm dead on my feet."

"Ah. Nonsense. You are perfect. But let us go before you fall down. Unless you would like me to carry you?" He winked.

She laughed. "No, I can make it."

They walked north, with Nick scampering a bit behind, toward a part of town that she wasn't as familiar with. Everything she'd needed thus far—the hardware store, the market, the clinic, city hall—had been south of her place, so she'd never gone farther north than to La Mela Verde. But as they walked, the streets became almost impossibly narrow, the buildings tighter and more pressed together, and the streets zigzagged in a way that looked like Tetris blocks trying to fit together. They made so many turns as they walked that Audrey was sure she'd have gotten lost, if it weren't for G.

G, on the other hand, walked the streets without paying any mind, as he chattered on about how his dessert menu was working out. A native of Mussomeli, he probably could've walked the route blindfolded. "And yes, all of the desserts are a big hit," he said proudly. "I have been selling out of everything. More people see them in the case and have been ordering them. It's good."

"That's great," she said, though right now, her mind was on other things.

"All because of you. If you hadn't given me your opinion, I don't know where I'd ..."

"Hmm," Audrey mumbled. "I'm so glad. Of course everything you make is amazing."

She took another few steps before she realized that G wasn't with her. When she stopped and turned around, he was standing still, staring at her. "Is everything okay?"

He smiled. "That is what I wonder about you. Your mind is very troubled. Am I wrong?"

She shook her head. "You're not. Sorry. First I found out my house was condemned. Then I learned the clinic was in violation, too, and now I can't use either place until I fix them. And then, with the inspector ..." She groaned. "I can't fix the clinic until the police clear the crime scene. Of course, people think I did it because I was frustrated over him giving me those citations. But really, if I were going to murder him, I wouldn't have left him in reception. I'd have found a smarter place to hide the body!"

Her voice had been steadily rising as she said that, and when they passed a man and a woman, strolling toward them, the couple eyed her suspiciously. She cleared her throat and spoke quietly. "I have no idea why his body wound up in my place. Absolutely none."

They'd walked to the end of a narrow alley. In America, a place like this would be where people kept their garbage cans. But G swerved her to a nondescript, windowless door, its paint chipping. It looked like an entrance to a speakeasy. He pulled it open and motioned for her to go in.

She peered inside to find, among the darkness, a faint reddish light, glowing from within, down a long hallway. She heard the faint chatter of voices coming from somewhere nearby. "After you," he said with a sweep of his hand.

Audrey eyed the passage and cringed. Nick paused there, too, and if *he* was wary, then there was big problem. This definitely looked like a place where some bad, illegal things went down. "What is this, a torture chamber?"

He laughed. "It is some of the most delicious meals in town. Other than mine, of course. Come."

She paused and knelt beside Nick. "You stay here. I'll bring you a treat."

G smiled down at the animal. "You have a faithful pet."

"He is indeed. Mostly because I give him the food."

"Oh, no. What gentleman in his right mind wouldn't want to spend all the time he can with you?"

She blushed. There he went again, with that Sicilian charm.

G took the lead, then, holding the door only long enough for her to pass through, then slipped his hand in hers and guided her down a narrow hallway with an uneven floor that seemed to tilt and rise as they walked. It opened up to a candlelit room, with a handful of people at tables, enjoying meals and talking. The place was a windowless wine cellar, bordered on two sides by a latticework of wine bottles. It should've felt cold and damp, but with that many bodies in such a small area, it was warm, and not uncomfortably so.

"G!" a stout man in a dirty apron shouted from across the room. He approached and gave G the double-cheek kiss. Then he said in Italian, "It is always an honor to have you." Audrey was happy that she could translate; it meant her language skills were indeed getting better.

G grinned. "It has been too long, yes?" He motioned to Audrey. "This is my guest, the lovely Dottore Audrey Smart. Audrey, this is Arturo, the best cook in Mussomeli, besides me. Arturo, my friend …Do you have a table for us?"

He chuckled. "For you? I have the best table in the place!"

He led them out of the room and placed them at a table that was away from the rest of the crowd, where there were giant barrels of wine. They were the only ones in the room. It was quiet there, and though the walls were stone and seemed to be weeping a bit, it was warm because of a large fireplace with a roaring fire. The table had a little handkerchief print tablecloth and tiny forget-me-nots in a bud vase, beside mismatched salt and pepper shakers. Quaint and rustic, it was definitely romantic, too.

Not that she was thinking about *that* in the least.

Arturo pulled out the chair and, when she sat, deposited a menu in her lap. He poured from a cask of red wine two glasses for them, without even asking. Audrey assumed it must've been the house wine. She took a sip of it and squinted at the menu, trying to read the choices in the dim firelight. Even in her limited Italian knowledge, everything looked so good.

"What do you recommend here?" she asked as Arturo left.

She looked up and noticed Arturo hadn't even given G a menu. He winked. "I always ask for his special. It's usually the best, no matter what it is."

She closed the menu. "Okay. Well, that makes it easy."

"So tell me," he said, leaning forward with his elbows on the table. "*Principessa*. What has been troubling you? The murder?"

She nodded. "And other things."

"You say both properties were condemned?"

"Well … not exactly condemned. They had their certificates of occupancy revoked until I can make repairs. So I was working on it. Luckily, the animals can stay in the clinic, because it was supposed to be a very quick fix. It's black mold. I arranged to have someone to fix it, but then the body of the inspector was found in my reception area. So now they're not letting anyone in or out except me, to care for the animals. And when I go in, I have to have a police escort, even just to feed and take care of them. So I have to make an appointment to do that. Can you believe that?" She grabbed her phone and started to jab something in. "Which reminds me. I have to make an appointment to check on those bunnies tonight."

"Bunnies?"

"Yes. Wild ones. They need a lot of care."

After all that, her throat was dry. She drained her wine glass and began to feel a little light-headed. Then she poked a message in to the detective. *Can I have an officer in the clinic at 8? I need to take care of the animals again.*

He came back with, *Someone will meet you there then.* She frowned at it. He'd been accommodating, but those poor animals. She hated having to make all those arrangements, just to go in and see them. It didn't feel right.

"You have had a busy week."

"Right. So I can't get the place back to normal, where I can see appointments and save strays and do what I was put here to do, until the police figure out who killed Vito Cascarelli. Time is of the essence. At least, for me, it is, if I want to keep the clinic running and not have to declare bankruptcy. And I get the feeling they're not working hard enough. Not to mention that they think I'm the one behind it, *again*."

"They can't think someone like—"

102

"G. Come on." She leveled a *get serious* look at him. "I may look like an innocent teenager, but that didn't stop them from suspecting me in the past."

He nodded slowly. "So what do you do now?"

"Since I can't work, obviously, I've been doing a little poking. Turns out the inspector was being forced to go really hard on expats, in order to keep them in compliance, and he was nearly having a mental breakdown, with how many COs he had to revoke. So there were a lot of people who were upset with him. Not just me. I went around and checked on a few of them, but all of them had alibis that checked out. Then I checked into the guy who stood to take on the inspector's job, once he was out of the way. But he was friends with Cascarelli; actually felt bad that he was dead. So it's probably not him, either. I'm at a dead end."

"You are?"

"Yes. I thought that maybe it was his ex-wife, since I read that there had been a recent divorce. Maybe it wasn't amicable, they got in a fight, and she stabbed him? But *why* in my place?"

"Yes, and why was he there to begin with?"

"I know. I didn't call him. But maybe someone did. My thought was that he was there to put a notice of the revocation of the certificate of occupancy on the door. There's a chance that Luca, the boy who was watching the place that day, left the door open, so it's possible the inspector went inside for some reason … I don't know why. But maybe the murderer was lying in wait, ready to attack!"

"Not Luca …?"

"Oh, no. Not him. That was just an accident. I think maybe someone came to see me, opened the door, and met him there. Maybe they had a discussion and it went south, and then whoever the killer was just decided to end him, right there. I do think it was a spur-of-the-moment, crime of passion thing. They used my letter opener!" She was babbling now, so fast that she could barely control her own tongue.

"Letter opener?" His eyes bulged.

She slumped back in her chair, trying to force away the memory of the last time she'd seen that letter opener. "This all could've been solved by now if I had cameras installed in reception. I was planning to, when I had the funds."

"Perhaps whoever did the crime saw that you had failed inspection, and is trying to—what's the word—picture you?"

"You mean frame me?" A shiver passed through her. "Maybe. That did cross my mind. But who? It's not like I have enemies."

"I don't think you need them. It might be that that person saw the notice, had the opportunity, and knew he could get away with it."

"Yes. That makes sense. But who?"

He pressed his lips together. "Maybe you should let the police handle it. So you don't get your pretty head in trouble? If a man commits murder, there is little to stop him from murdering again to conceal the first crime. You could be in danger. Yes?"

She rolled her eyes. "Like I said, I can't wait. I have to get that clinic open. Not just for me but for the animals. For the town. Before I moved here, everyone was telling me how important it was to get those animals off the street. Now, no one seems to care how much they suffer."

"A man did die."

"Yes, I know." Was she sounding insensitive? Yes, probably. But sometimes she got that way. Sometimes she held the plight of animals over that of her fellow human beings.

Arturo came back and refilled her wine glass. She eagerly took another sip. Now it was going down like water, and she felt even more lightheaded, probably the result of her empty stomach. G ordered two specials, which she was glad of, because her mouth was full of wine.

G watched her with concern. "You may want to go easy on the wine."

She sighed. "I need something to relax me. I'm so jittery. Probably because I haven't had any sleep."

"No?" He inspected her closely. "Where have you been sleeping lately? You stay in a hotel?"

She held her wine glass to her lips. "Oh, um. Not—"

"I don't let you stay in a hotel! Not my friends! No, you come and stay with me. I have a nice, comfortable room, just for you!"

She almost choked on the sip of wine in her mouth. "Actually, no. I'm already staying with … I already have a place to stay, so I'm fine."

"Oh? With who?" He leaned forward, the sparkle in his eye a challenge.

" A … friend."

One of his eyebrows arched. "A friend?"

"Yeah, um …" She looked away awkwardly. "Just a friend. You probably know him. Mason, the contractor? I think you've met him."

G's eyes sparked with recognition, but it wasn't the good kind. It was as if she'd mentioned a particular ingredient he wasn't very fond of, because he seemed to clench his teeth a bit. Did that mean he didn't like the man? Or that he didn't like the man *with her?* "Ah."

She added quickly, "He's, like I said, just a friend."

"Ah. I see." He sipped his wine. "That is good. As long as you are taken care of, with this friend of yours. Then ... what will you do?"

She shrugged. "What do you think I should do?"

"I would take this time to work on your own place, *si?* Consider it a blessing and fix it up so you can stop staying with this *friend* of yours, eh? And at least get back into your own place and get a good night's sleep."

Yep. No doubt. He was definitely a little peeved about the Mason thing. But if he was, why didn't he make his move? What was he waiting for?

She nodded slowly. Moving out of Mason's sounded like the sane plan. The safe plan. And yet ...

She wrinkled her nose.

He laughed. "You think something else?"

"I think I should probably go around and check all the other houses with notices on the doors. Maybe that way, I can find someone who had a beef with Vito Cascarelli and would want to see him dead."

"Sounds like a bit of a ... um, a cat chasing its tail?"

She sighed and polished off her second glass of wine, even before the food arrived. Now, she really felt woozy. Woozy, but ... undaunted. Fearless. Determined. "It's not so bad. I mean, I have plenty of time, since I'm not working. And I have been meaning to get out there and see more of the city. It'll be like exploring."

"Maybe, but you do not know the city. It could be dangerous."

She waved that away. "Bah. What could happen?"

At that moment, Arturo arrived with their food, as well as bread and a slurry of olive oil full of fresh spices. The plate in front of her contained some rolled fishy gray things, bursting with breadcrumbs. She'd been hungry before, but the pungent, salty scent of the seafood turned her stomach. She set her wine glass down, and when Arturo dutifully went to fill it, she put a hand over it. "Could I have a glass of water instead?"

"Of course."

He went off to get it and she stared at the food. "What is this?"

"*Sarde a beccafico*," G said, quickly polishing off the first one. "Delicious. Sardines stuffed with pine nuts, raisins, breadcrumbs, parmesan. An island specialty. You try!"

He pointed at her plate with her fork, but that description had her stomach turning even more. Raisins and sardines? No thanks.

But he was staring at her, expectant.

"Oh ... I'm ..." She took a little bit in her fork and tasted. It was, in a word, weird. She could definitely taste the raisins. And the sardines. "Yum."

"I tell you, you like it."

She took another bite. It actually wasn't terrible. Nothing in Sicily was. The more she ate, the more she liked it. He was still watching her, and she wanted to please him. He was a good man, listening to all of her problems, offering suggestions and advice. Mason would've likely replied with some kind of joke, or teased her. But not G. He was actually trying to help.

In fact, this whole meal had been, at this point, all about her and her many problems. She needed to show him how much she appreciated him. This. All of it.

"It is really good. And this is really a great place. Thanks for taking me here." She grabbed at the breadbasket on the table and found a slice of crusty bread. She dipped it in the olive oil and took a bite. "Mmm. Good bread."

At least it would sop up some of the alcohol in her stomach.

G tilted his head at her. "You're going to the clinic after this?"

She nodded.

His gaze turned deadly serious. "You should be very careful. You know that there is one other possibility."

"Like what?"

"That it was dark, and the person who murdered the inspector thought it was you."

A chill went down her back. "That's ridiculous. Like I said, I don't have any enemies! Besides, I'm going to have a police officer meeting me there."

For the first time, she was actually glad of that. Because as G's words echoed in her ears, she had to admit, she really didn't know. Was someone trying to kill her? If so, why?

Arturo arrived with her glass of water. She said, "More wine, please," hoping for the first time that the police did meet her at the clinic. If not, who knew who else would be there, waiting for her?

106

CHAPTER EIGHTEEN

As they left the restaurant, Audrey felt like she was floating on air.

She was a lot tipsier than she was used to. But she only realized the fact when they arrived at G's café, and G let go of her arm and she had to physically brace her knees so they wouldn't buckle under her.

"I should walk you home," G said.

"Don't be silly." She smiled toothily up at him, batted her eyelashes as winsomely as she could. "I'm fine. Besides. I've got to go to the clinic, remember? The police will be there."

"*Si*, but you don't seem to be in any condition to—"

"I'm okay! Really!"

Here she was, looking up at him on this romantic, moonlit night, practically begging for a kiss, and he wanted to talk about her safety? What a letdown. What happened to the moon hitting her eye like a big pizza pie?

Seriously, did she need him to spell it out for her? He wasn't interested.

"I'm fine," she said, smiling again. "Besides, I'll be totally fine. I have Nick, who is not only a faithful pet, but he once saved my life. He's totally fierce."

"All right, *Principessa*." His eyes were definitely full of worry, not *amore*. "You take care of yourself, now."

Audrey toddled along the street, heading toward the clinic, thinking. What the heck was wrong with her? One minute, she was practically drooling over Mason, and the next, she wanted G to kiss her? No wonder she didn't have either one of them wrapped around her finger. She was a waffler, and completely fouling this up. She deserved to have a love life that was a total train wreck. Brina would be so disappointed.

As she walked down the empty, dark pathways lit only by the dim, sparse streetlamps, she thought back to her conversation with G at dinner, and started to feel a little worried. *Does someone want to kill me? If so, who?*

The thought marinated in her head, making her stop and turn around every few steps. Every time she did, Nick let out a little whimper, wanting her to continue on. She'd brought him a bit of the sardine-raisin dish as a treat, but he hadn't been a fan either. Now, he was irritated.

I'm being paranoid, she thought as she walked toward the main road in town. When she got there, she breathed a sigh of relief, because there were many people there, in the center of the city, listening to a man playing an accordion near the fountain. A few drunk young people were dancing to the music.

She didn't stop to listen. She had too much on her mind.

The moment she rounded the corner and headed toward the clinic, she found waiting for her Officer Ricci, the young, buff officer whom she knew quite well. She tried to wave at him, but the floor seemed to be tilting. Her arms flailed as she struggled for balance.

She paused, propping herself up against a telephone pole to wait. It was really warm now, and she couldn't breathe. The air felt like a physical object, heavy, weighing down on her. Also, the scenery seemed to want to spin around her. She blinked.

Ricci came running up to her. "Eh … you okay? Sit."

He guided her and sat her down on the stoop of the building next door, while she took a few breaths. Yes, four glasses of wine was more than she was used to, but she'd felt fine when she left the restaurant and got out in the fresh air. She blinked and stood up. "Sorry. I'm good. Guess I just had a little too much wine at dinner."

With his help, she walked to the door. He took aside the yellow crime scene tape and let her go in. She did her best to ignore the spot where Vito Cascarelli's body had lain, sidestepping around it as she went to the animals. A few times, she touched the walls on either side of her, as if on a ship at high seas.

As she went through her regular routine, she had to brace herself against the counter a few times to keep from falling over. This was not good. She fought to keep herself upright, blinking her eyes. Then she poured herself a cup of water and guzzled it. Better. Sort of. Well, not really. Now, her stomach hurt.

Ricci watched her from the door. "Everything all right, *Dottore?*"

She smiled and patted his hard chest, admiring how well-built it was, then realized that sober Dr. Smart never would do that. "Uh, fine. I'm almost done here. If you want to help, the food for the cats is over there?"

He crouched down, following her pointed finger, and dragged out the giant bag of dry cat food, then started to fill the dishes. Meanwhile, the animals were going crazy, their barking and whimpering so shrill to her ears, it hurt. They had every right to be antsy—though she'd been in twice to see to the bunnies, the other animals hadn't had their daily exercise today. Maybe she'd come in tomorrow and give them a good workout, if the officer would let her.

"So," she said casually as she checked on the bunnies. They were all doing well, their eyes open, and now, they seemed to be moving much more, exploring the incubator. She picked one up and started to feed it with the prepared formula. "How is the investigation into the inspector's death going?"

Ricci shrugged. "Slow. We follow tips. But not many of them. I think the detective doesn't know anything just yet."

Great. That was not what she wanted to hear. "So he doesn't have any suspects?"

Ricci filled a cat dish and looked at her sheepishly. "Well ... you."

Oh, even better. "There has to be more. Doesn't he have any leads at all? I mean, I wasn't the only one the inspector flunked, right? The man has to have plenty of enemies."

"Yes. But I spent all today looking into that list. All good. All checked out. I interview all people around this area at that time. No one see anything. Someone see the inspector go in, but no one see them go out, or anyone else there. So!" He threw up his hands. "It's a big mystery."

"What time did he go in?"

"Around nine."

"I was coming home from Agrigento at that point. Mason Legare can vouch for that," she said. "I told DiNardo that."

"*Si*, but no one knows when he was murdered. It may have been much after that."

Audrey sighed. "That's great. Just wonderful." She finished with the bunnies and reached in to pet old Bruno's fur. "Do you know what else he's doing?"

"No. Just that he is doing everything he can. DiNardo really try."

She groaned. Yes, he probably was. He was a good detective. Unfortunately, with her livelihood on the line, he could've been Superman, and it wouldn't have been enough. She wanted to be cleared of this crime and get on with her life, now.

"I know. And I know you are doing everything possible, too." She patted his arm, feeling how massive and solid it was, and then realized Sober Audrey probably wouldn't have done that either.

She said goodbye and walked up to the front of the clinic with Ricci dutifully watching her every move. He opened the door to let her pass through. When she reached for the light switch, she accidentally glanced at the spot where the dead man had lain, and the dizziness overcame her. Everything started to swirl and her gut twisted. Suddenly, she lost her balance and found herself falling …

Right into Ricci's arms.

He caught her, almost as if this were a dance and he was dipping her, so that they were face to face, with very little space between them. She giggled. "Oh. Whoops."

Ricci started to lift her back on her feet, but his attention was caught by a figure, standing still on the sidewalk. Audrey followed his line of sight to …

Mason.

CHAPTER NINETEEN

She scrambled to get herself up. "Oh. Hi, Mason. What are you doing here?"

"Just came to see if you need help," he mumbled, his voice guarded. "But it looks like you're doing just fine."

He turned to leave.

"Oh. Thanks!" She nudged Ricci away and bounded down the steps toward Mason. She turned to make sure Ricci was closing and locking the door and putting up the yellow tape, and as she whirled she stumbled backwards into Mason. "Whoops."

Luckily, he took ahold of her at the last minute and helped her straighten. "Whoa." When she righted herself, he said, still in that guarded way, "Are you okay?"

"Totally!" she said, waving at Ricci. "The officer had to escort me as I took care of the animals. Because of the murder, you know. So I'm done. I'm ready to go home. Thanks, Officer."

She knew she was babbling but couldn't stop herself. The streets were spinning. She wasn't sure how far she went before Mason clamped a hand on her arm, dragging her in a different direction than the one she'd been headed in. Where was she? Everything seemed foreign. She giggled. *That's because you're in a foreign country, dummy.*

"What happened to you, girl? You been drinking?"

Oh. Well, I had a glass or two. Or three, or four, at dinner?" She let out a girlish giggle that she didn't know she was capable of. The stars overhead were spinning around her.

"Dinner?"

She was so busy marveling at the stars all around and fumbling for her answer that she didn't watch where she was going. Suddenly, a curb jumped out in front of her, and she went stumbling, nearly falling like a house of cards in the middle of the street.

"Whoa," Mason said, lifting her to her feet.

She stared up at him. God, he was so beautiful. It should be a crime to make anyone that gorgeous, with his cinnamon hair catching the moonlight, flopping in his face. His blue eyes were dark now, but

111

focused on her intensely. That jawbone of his could cut diamonds. In Hollywood, talent scouts would be swarming all over him. No doubt. She licked her lips, wondering what it would be like to kiss him, when …

"Girl, you're a mess," he muttered, then leaned down. Was he going to … would he finally … and then she could tell Brina she'd finally experienced her first romantic kiss in Sicily?

She closed her eyes, waiting for that pressure on her lips.

It never came.

She was confused for about a second. When she opened her eyes again, everything started to spin even faster. She lost control of her feet, her balance, and thought for sure she was going to hit the cold ground. But then she realized she was suddenly weightless, being lifted into the air. Mason's arms wrapped around her, holding her to his hard chest.

She looked up at him, stunned. Not a kiss, but still. This was … really romantic. Wasn't it? Like he was her knight in shining armor. She stared up at him, at the stubble on that strong jaw of his, as he easily traversed the street, not pausing to look down at her. "What are you doing?" she asked breathlessly.

She'd been expecting something like, *I cannot bear to see thou in distress, milady. Wilt thou accept my offer of assistance?* Instead, he muttered, "I didn't want to see you splattered on the ground, Hot Mess."

At that point, Audrey decided she'd probably regret this tomorrow.

But at that moment, she didn't care. She pressed the side of her face against his warm chest, inhaling the scent of his detergent mixed with a spicy aftershave, and sighed happily. For the first time in a long time, she felt safe. Taken care of.

"You're kind of cute when you're playing my hero, Abs," she whispered sleepily, nestling up against him.

"Uh-huh. Right. You sound like that sister of yours."

"Oh. I've got to call Brina."

"I think the only thing you've got to do is have some water, an aspirin, and a good night's sleep."

It seemed only a second later that the door to his place opened and she was deposited on his nice, fluffy sofa, among all the chenille pillows. She settled into them, feeling like she was floating on a cloud. Happy. Perfect. The specter of the murder and all her worries about her properties seemed so very far away, unable to touch or harm her.

A glass of cold water and a pill were deposited in her hand. Mechanically, she popped the pill, sucked down the water. "Thank you, kind sir," she slurred.

"You ain't gonna hurl, are you, Boston?" Mason's disembodied voice said, as if echoing from a thousand miles away.

She wanted to shake her head, but she was already mostly asleep.

*

It was the same dream, just as always. Her father, in his flannel shirt and work boots, walking from room to room. She smiled at the smell of sawdust and fresh paint as she spun in an enormous circular room, part of a turret in a Queen Anne Victorian. The windows gave a gorgeous three-sixty view of the city skyscrapers, the Back Bay, and the rest of the stately Boston brownstones in the neighborhood. The sun shone in, making her feel warm, as seagulls cried overhead.

"Dad, this is the nicest one yet," she said to him. "I love it."

He laughed. "You'd like to live here someday, huh?"

She nodded greedily, imagining this her bedroom. Brina could have one of the many bedrooms downstairs. But this one, on the third floor, was the nicest. She could just imagine her white canopy bed, right in that corner, surrounded by windows. It'd be so—

A floorboard creaked. With a start, she realized her dad had left her.

She rushed forward to find him in the doorway, right near the steps. She reached for his hand, but he pulled away and fished in the breast pocket of his flannel, pulling out a cigarette.

"Dad, don't—"

"I know, I know. Don't smoke in here." He smiled and tucked the cigarette back.

Of course, that wasn't what she'd wanted to say. *Don't leave.* But for some reason, her mouth wasn't allowing her to get the words out.

He went down the stairs, and she followed him, trying to keep up.

This time, as she followed him, she tried again. She slipped her hand in his, expecting to feel the warmth, the calluses from all the hard work he did, but the hand faded. She realized she was holding air.

"Dad!" she cried, her heart in her throat, knowing he was about to disappear. "Please."

"Don't be afraid. You have it right there." He winked at her and pointed at her hands.

She realized she was holding that folded piece of cardstock, the postcard he'd kept in his pocket. She gazed at the warm sunset, all those pink and orange tropical colors, melting together over the still dark water. The black mountain range. In it, she noticed a house she'd never seen before. She could only see the outline of it, but a window was ablaze with light. In it, the silhouettes of two people were there, looking out, possibly stargazing.

She stared at the postcard wistfully, as her father took it from her hands. "You like that? Someday, we'll go there. It's called Montagnanera."

"Yes! Dad?"

But he was falling away suddenly, fading like a vapor into the air. She reached for him, and to her horror, her hand passed right through his body.

"No!"

She woke up to a heavy heart, thudding uncomfortably in her chest.

Her eyes slowly opened and she realized why. Nick was standing on her chest, peering down at her curiously.

"Ow," she mumbled, shoving him off. "Move move move *move*."

He scampered off of her body to the carpet as she threw off the blankets. As she did, she found a little trash bin had been propped next to her pillow. Mason's work, obviously.

Bits and pieces of last night came back to her as she rushed to grab a pen and paper from her purse. She found a couple business cards, but no pen, just a dried-up tube of lipstick she never wore and a roll of Lifesavers. Tossing those down, she quickly picked up her phone, opened it to the "Notes" section, and wrote down *Montagnanera*.

She sighed, feeling better having gotten that out.

That was the place. The place her father had loved. The place he had longed to escape to. The place he'd dreamed about. *Montagnanera*. She said the name, over and over again, then entered it into the search bar on her phone.

A bunch of results came back, but none seemed quite right. No places, at least. Most were for an indie rock band from Europe that had had one hit in the 1990s.

Hmm. Had she spelled it wrong? She entered in a number of possible letter combinations, trying to find a town or city or country or landmark that had the name, but all she saw were pictures of a bunch of guys with big hair. She tossed her phone down in frustration as her eyes went to the trash bin sitting beside her couch.

114

Audrey winced as she remembered curling up in Mason's arms, sniffing his T-shirt like some kind of insane person. Yes, it had been quite lovely, how well she'd fit into his arms, against his body, but she hadn't meant to announce it to the world. She'd done that, right? And had she also called him Abs?

Oh, my. I want to bury myself in the backyard and never come out.

And then he'd brought her back here and thrown her down on the couch. What had he called her? Not gorgeous. Not lovely. Not charming or winsome or any of those things.

He'd called her a hot mess.

And right then, she felt like one. Her mouth felt like she'd swallowed a cactus and her head throbbed. Not to mention, she felt a little like …

She grabbed the trash can and held it there in her lap, wondering if she was going to be sick.

But nothing came out.

Yes, she was definitely a hot mess.

Just then, she heard footsteps on the staircase above her. She threw her blankets over her head and pretended to be asleep. She didn't want to face Mason.

Luckily, she didn't have to. She could feel him hovering in the doorway, but a moment later, he opened the front door and disappeared.

The second the door clicked closed, she sat up. Time to go back to the clinic and decide where to look for answers next.

CHAPTER TWENTY

Having popped two Excedrin, Audrey successfully avoided Mason, who must've gone for his morning run with Polpetto, and rushed to the clinic, going over the details of the case in her head. Though she'd hoped the medicine would've helped with the headache, by the time she got to the main square in town, her head was spinning with all the possibilities, and the dull throb hadn't gone away.

Plus, she still felt a little nauseated.

But the second she got to the clinic and saw the yellow tape, she felt worse. Once again, she'd forgotten to ask the police to come so they could escort her inside.

Groaning, she quickly texted DiNardo. *I'm here and I need someone to escort me into the clinic.*

No response. This was getting to be a big pain in the butt.

She crossed her arms, tapping her foot impatiently. Those poor doggies. They were probably dying for someone to take them for a walk.

She was just about to type in another message to him, this one in all caps, when a car pulled to the curb in front of her.

An older woman with dark curly hair streaked with gray popped out and started to scream at her in Italian, gesturing wildly.

"Whoa. Slow down! I don't speak Italian very ..."

The woman didn't slow down. At first, Audrey wondered if she'd done something wrong, but then she realized the woman was more scared than upset, and pointing at something in the back of her car. When she heard the word *veterinaria,* she understood.

"Yes, I'm the veterinarian. What can I help you with?" she asked, rushing to the car and peering in the window.

The woman continued to shout, something about her car and an animal. Audrey didn't have to understand every word to know what had happened. The poor yellow-striped cat was lying on its side in the back of the car, in obvious pain. The fur on one paw was matted with blood, and the leg was bent awkwardly.

"Oh, poor thing!" Audrey sighed, looking up and down the street. No police.

Yes, she wasn't supposed to go inside without a police escort. But this was an emergency, and she couldn't stand to see the animal in pain. She reached into her bag and pulled out her keys, pushed aside the yellow tape, and opened the door.

"Okay. Bring her right this way," she said, motioning to the woman.

The woman opened the back of the car, scooped the animal up, and carried her in. "Thank you. Thank you so much."

"Oh. You speak English?" *Why didn't you say that before, lady?*

She nodded as she ushered her back into surgery and helped her settle the animal down on the table. Audrey could tell the hind leg had been clipped and was bleeding, but it didn't look all that bad.

"Poor girl's probably just shaken up. I don't think it's broken," she said. "What's her name?"

The woman looked around the place as if she'd entered a new dimension, with a mix of horror and fear. "Oh. She is not mine. I was driving into town to take care of some things, and she came out of nowhere. I couldn't stop in time. My car hit her."

"I understand," she said, opening up a drawer and pulling out a clipboard. "Could I just have you fill this out?"

She stared at it warily. "I'm not going to have to ... pay for any of this?"

"Oh. No. It's just standard procedure. I'm very thankful that you brought her to me. Most people wouldn't have the decency to that these days, unfortunately." Audrey pointed to the paper. "Just the top part. You don't need to fill out the bottom."

The woman's hands shook as she wrote her name. Poor woman. She was obviously as shaken by the incident as the cat. She was probably late forties, her tanned skin marred with age spots that suggested a love of sunbathing. Audrey watched her, having a sudden feeling of déjà vu. Had she met this woman before?

The little cat was more alert now, and mewling slightly as Audrey felt the injury. Just as she'd suspected, the bone wasn't broken, just bruised. Audrey took some gauze and started to wrap up the injury in a splint. "I think she'll be fine. No collar, so likely another stray, but I'll check for a chip. We'll keep her and monitor her until she gets better."

The woman didn't look up. "Is ... this the room where the body was found?"

Audrey nearly choked, she was so stunned by the question. "Um ... excuse me?"

117

Her eyes went to the form. There, on the first line, was the name: CASCARELLI, LISA.

It was Vito's ex-wife.

She stared at her, still trying to comprehend. This was the woman Audrey had worried was Vito's murderer. It was possible, definitely, considering that marital fights could often escalate. And the divorce was fresh. It seemed like more than a coincidence that she'd show herself here, so soon after his death. Was she so deranged that she'd ... hit a cat just so she could come in here and poke around? See how things were going with the investigation?

Talk about ... warped.

"Um, well—"

"Did you find my husband's body?"

Audrey nodded. "Yes. As for where the body was found ..." *If she murdered him, she'd know exactly where she left the body.* "No. Actually. It was in the room with the animals," she lied.

"Oh. Can I see?"

She winced. Why the heck would this woman want to see where her husband died? Talk about morbid. *Good thinking, Audrey. You brought the murderer back to the scene of the crime. The police are going to skin you alive.* "Unfortunately, we really shouldn't be in here at all. It's a crime scene. I'm kind of breaking the law right now. But ..." She motioned to the poor cat. "I felt like this was an emergency."

"Hmm." The woman eyed her skeptically. "When you found him, what was he like?"

Was this a trick question? "Uh ... dead." The woman gave her a sour look. "I mean, he had been murdered that night, and I was freaking out, so I didn't get a very good look at him. I just saw that he was dead and called the police. I'm very sorry for your loss."

Lisa Cascarelli shrugged. "It was sad, of course. We'd been married many years. But Vito was not a real man, you know? Not very macho. He had no backbone. I was surprised he took the job that Tomas offered, knowing what I knew of him. He didn't like to fight. I was the one who divorced him. Found a real man and told him it was over." She shook her head. "It was a surprise when the police showed up at my door yesterday. He didn't deserve this. No. Not at all."

"So you cared about him?" Audrey asked.

The woman laughed bitterly. "I was married to him for nineteen years. Of course I did. I didn't want him dead. What I can't understand is how this could've happened to him. He was a nice man. Did not want

118

to ruffle feathers. His job made him do that. He only took it for the money."

"You don't think he had any enemies?"

"Of course not," Lisa said, running her long fingernails through her curly mane of hair. "He would be the last person I'd expect this to happen to. When I heard of it, I thought maybe he was mugged, had his wallet stolen. Mussomeli is a safe place, but with all the new people coming in... who knows? But then I find out that he was found in a veterinarian office? It makes no sense to me. Do *you* know?"

The woman's eyes were slit in suspicion.

"No. I mean, I knew him. He inspected my properties. Failed them, too, but I understood. I was just as shocked as anyone to find him. I liked him. He seemed, like you said, like a nice man."

"Oh, he was. Almost too nice for his own good," she said, her eyes volleying around the place. "You say he failed this clinic?"

"Yes. He did, the day before he died. I think the reason he was here was because he was putting a sign on the door. But one of the dog walkers I use had left the door open. And for some reason he went in. I've been thinking about it over and over again and I don't know why he would have. Maybe someone lured him in there, or called him, pretending to be me ..." She sighed and added, earnestly, "I do wish we could find out what happened. Until we can, I can't get this place open, and all of my animals are in jeopardy."

"Hmmm," she said. That seemed to appease her. "That is a shame."

Audrey finished her wrapping and petted the cat's soft yellow head. "I wish I could tell you more. Did you come here hoping to get some clues as to what happened?"

"No. But I knew where this place was. I Googled it when Vito died. So when I hit the cat I knew exactly where to go," she said with a sheepish smile. "That was lucky."

Audrey nodded. It certainly was.

"I came in from Sutera to speak with his lawyers. I'm still listed on all his papers as his next-of-kin. I must settle his affairs." She checked her wristwatch. "Which reminds me! I must go!"

Audrey placed the animal in a bed and said, "Well, don't worry about this kitty. I think she's going to be just fine. I will look after her."

"*Grazie*," the woman said, rushing to the door. With her hand on the doorknob, she turned. "I know what you must be thinking. But I cared about Vito. Didn't even want the alimony from him. Like I said, he was a good man. A saint, in a lot of ways. Sometimes I wish I would have treated him better."

Audrey nodded. "I understand."

"Again, thank you for your help," she said with a smile. "You are a good doctor."

As Audrey watched her get into her car and leave, she mentally scrubbed "the ex-wife" off her possible list of suspects. Lisa Cascarelli was either a fantastic liar, or she didn't know what had happened to her husband.

That meant that somewhere out there, a murderer was running free. A shiver went down Audrey's spine as she stepped outside and started to reattach the crime scene tape. Now she wasn't just a *suspected* felon. If the police knew what she was up to, she'd probably get arrested. She had to figure out what was going on. Soon.

"What are you doing?" a voice said behind her.

Her entire body went stiff. She knew that voice.

It was Detective DiNardo.

CHAPTER TWENTY ONE

"Hi, Detective!" she said brightly, smiling at him, hoping to disguise the fact that her heart was beating a million miles an hour and she was sweating now. "How are you? What's new with the case?"

He frowned back, motioning at the door with his chin. "Did you go in there? After I specifically told you not to?"

"Well, you see ..." She tittered. "Funny story, I—"

"It's not that funny. Especially considering that it's grounds for me to arrest you. Tampering with a—"

She threw up her hands. "I couldn't help it! Detective ... I messaged you ..." She pulled out her phone and stared at it. "Twenty-six minutes ago. I needed to get in there. It was an emergency."

"Perhaps, but I told you that under no circumstance were you to—"

"But a cat got hit by a car!" she shouted in her defense, gesturing wildly toward Lisa Cascarelli's car, which was no longer parked in the spot outside her clinic. "I didn't want it bleeding to death out here. Sue me for actually having a heart and doing what I've been trained to do, which is putting the care and health of animals over all else."

He fell silence, his lips pinched. Then he motioned to the door. "Show me."

The request came as a surprise to Audrey. "What?"

"I'd like to see the cat that was hit by the car."

Of course, he didn't trust her. And for good reason. Audrey let out an exasperated huff. At least she could show him the wounded animal, gain some of that trust back. What did he expect her to do? Ignore the poor thing? Really. How heartless did he think she could be?

"Fine." She marched inside, to the surgery. The door was partly open, but she pushed it wide, letting him go through. "There."

He looked in, his dark eyes scanning the room. "Where?"

"There. Obviously. In the bed in the corner."

He squinted for a moment. "What am I looking at?"

Confused, she peered in, standing on her tiptoes to look over his shoulder. Oh no. This wasn't right at all. She was sure she'd left the wounded cat in that bed, to recover...

But now, the cat was gone.

Her heart stopped for a full ten seconds. Then, frantic, she broke into spastic action, scanning the room, the hallway. No cat. She even squatted to look under the exam table. A little part of her brain wondered what it would feel like to be snapped into handcuffs, and if the jail cells downtown were as horrible as they appeared on television shows. "She was just here! A yellow tabby cat with an injured paw. You have to believe me! I was just waiting outside, like a good citizen, for the police to arrive, when she came and—"

"Hold on. Hold on. Calm down," he said, putting his hands up.

But she couldn't. She was speaking a mile a minute, spittle flying from her mouth. Maybe this was the result of her going crazy. Or she was still hung over from last night. Could the cat have been some weird figment of her imagination? Maybe. She babbled, "Of course. I think I might have lost it. It was rather a big coincidence that Vito Cascarelli's wife just showed up out of nowhere …"

"Wait. Vito Cascarelli's wife showed up here with her cat?"

"No. Not *her* cat."

"So …some random cat?"

"Right."

"That's a coincidence."

"Right? That's just what I said."

"Okay. Back up. Let's start this from the beginning. You were waiting outside when … Lisa Cascarelli drove up with a cat?"

She nodded, then dragged her hands down her face. "Oh! No, I don't think I'm going insane. I really did treat that animal. I'm sure of it." Her head was starting to pound. She vised her head in her hands. "I need air."

"Come with me," he said. He led her down the hallway to the break room and sat her down, then fed her a little paper cup of water from the tap. She sipped it greedily, letting her breathing return to normal. When she looked up again, DiNardo was watching her, his face equal parts suspicion and concern. He stooped to her level. "Better?"

She nodded, feeling a little like a drama queen. Collecting her thoughts, she started again. "I'm sorry. I did treat a cat here. And by coincidence it was brought in by Mrs. Cascarelli. She'd hit it on her way into town. But she didn't touch anything, and neither did I. I just needed to bring the cat inside to take care of it. It had a twisted leg, but other than that … it must be fine because it's gone now. But it's got to be around here …" She twisted to peer under the table. "Somewhere?"

He nodded slowly. "All right."

"And I'm guessing from the way you're doubting absolutely every word I say that you have no more leads and I'm still the main suspect?" she asked.

He pulled out a chair and sat down across from her. "Unfortunately, we do not have much to go on. We did meet with Mrs. Cascarelli, and she checked out. She was in Palermo with her boyfriend at the time. We met with a couple of other people who the inspector had failed, but none of it got us any closer to finding out who did this."

"Meaning that I'm screwed, big-time," she muttered, slumping over the table. "And ... you're probably going to have to arrest me, right? You have grounds to, now. I trespassed on a crime scene."

He shook his head. "Hold on. Yes, you went against my explicit orders. But arresting you is not on my agenda right—"

"You probably should. It's not like my life could get any worse. I mean, at least, if you do that, I'll have a place to spend the night and won't have to be begging people for a spot on their couch. And they get three square meals in there, right? Without my clinic generating money for me to live on, I might not be able to do that for myself, soon." She stuck her lower lip out.

"Calm down, calm down. Look," he said. "I came down here myself to tell you that we've gotten everything we needed from the place and that it's no longer an active crime scene. So—"

"Wait. What?" What was this, a blink of good news in the middle of all the bad? "You mean I'm allowed into the clinic without an escort?"

"Now you are, yes."

"Really?" She clapped her hands. "Amazing! Thank you! Wait ..." Suddenly something occurred to her. "Why were you sounding the alarm and freaking out about my going inside the clinic, then? I thought I was—"

"Because it was up to *me* to tell you that. You knew the rules, and you went against them."

She sighed, the weight of his disapproving glare more like that of a father berating his daughter. "Okay. Fine. I'm sorry. But I did it for the cat."

"Right. The cat." He rolled his eyes to the ceiling. It was clear from his face that he still didn't believe her. "Anyway, I did want to let you know that as soon as possible so that you could start seeing clients again."

She pressed her lips together. "Can't. I still have the black mold problem." She grabbed for her phone. "But at least Mason can try to fix it now. I have to text him right away. And maybe I can go to city hall and see if they'll appeal the decision, in the meantime? I bet they're backed up on inspections. It's worth a shot, right?"

DiNardo shrugged and stood up. "I guess you need to do what you have to do," he said. "In order to keep the clinic rolling and getting yourself paying customers, I would say you have nothing to lose."

She was about to stand up, too, when she felt something brush up against her leg. She pushed away from the table to look at it when the yellow cat jumped into her lap, meowing excitedly. Grinning broadly, she pointed to its splint. "The cat, DiNardo. See? I told you."

He stared at it, his astonishment giving way to a smile. "All right, all right. But next time, Doctor ... Try to follow the rules?"

"I always *try*," she said.

He rolled his eyes and opened his mouth as if he was going to argue, but then clamped it closed, likely deciding it wasn't worth his time. She followed him outside, petting the injured cat in her arms as he tore the yellow crime scene tape from the door.

"Thanks for coming by," she called after him. "Finally!"

He paused to turn back and grimace at her. "I'm serious, Audrey. You know you are still our main suspect."

Right. He wouldn't let her forget it.

When DiNardo left, she quickly jabbed in a text to Mason: *Operation GET RID OF MOLD in effect. I'll leave the key under the doormat in case I'm not here when you get here.* Then she rushed to take care of the animals. She had to get to city hall. This clinic needed to open. Time to get things rocking and rolling.

CHAPTER TWENTY TWO

Audrey bought an apple from the corner market, took one bite, and gave the rest to her little friend. Nick stopped scampering alongside her to enjoy his treat. She waited for him, tapping her foot. "Come along, bub. We've got to get to city hall."

She rushed across the street to the main square, crossing past the fountain, where a number of people were sitting around on the green or on the benches, enjoying the beautiful morning weather. From the brightly colored banners hung over the square, it also appeared that there was a parade going on, too, to honor a feast day for *Madonna dei Miracoli.* A band was practicing in the alley and some ladies in bright-colored skirts and dresses were gathered together. Among the crowds, Audrey noticed Mayor Fanelli, standing at a grandstand in the corner of the square, testing a microphone.

A couple of children were skipping rope and someone was handing out flyers for a new restaurant opening up on the corner. Audrey took a flyer, glanced at it, folded it, and stuck it in the pocket of her jeans as she reached the steps of city hall, sighing. If she had less on her mind, she'd have loved to join in the festival, check out the new restaurant. But not now.

As she climbed the stairs, she crossed fingers on both hands, running over her little spiel in her mind. *The black mold is being taken care of. We are working toward bringing the clinic up to code right now. But the animals in the clinic and the city are suffering and need me in there, operating under normal hours.*

By the time she pulled open the door, she was fired up. She marched down the hall, toward the Building Inspector's Office, room 134, fists clenched and ready to attack.

Of course, when she got there, the door was closed. The building was empty, likely due to the parade going on outside.

She knocked on the door, tried the handle, and sighed. It was locked. She spun and stopped a young, twenty-something man in a suit. "Excuse me. Do you know where Inspector Dellisanti is?"

"Not here."

Ha. Very astute. "Is he at the parade?"

"Nope. Probably doing inspections. He's never in the office during the week. Only on Fridays." The man sped off without waiting for thanks or a follow-up question.

Audrey sighed and meandered down the hallway, toward the mayor's office. As she walked, she thought about what they'd been discussing right before they'd dissolved into chatter about vacations. It was something about revitalization efforts being ruined by Cascarelli. Dellisanti had come up clean, but what about the mayor?

He had a motive, too. If Cascarelli was pushing back on the mayor's efforts to make himself look good, maybe there'd been some kind of friction there. Maybe she needed to look into him more closely.

Outside, a microphone screeched, and someone, likely the mayor, began to speak. Audrey gnawed on her lip. Yes, she just got done telling Detective DiNardo she'd be sure to play by the rules, but when would she *ever* get such a perfect opportunity like this one?

Before she could think twice about it, she gripped the handle. It turned, and she easily slipped inside, closing the door behind her.

When she was in the massive, darkened office, she let out a breath of relief. She could totally do this. Even though she'd been in this office before, it'd been for such a brief time that she hadn't had a chance to look around. Large paintings loomed over her, full of pictures of distinguished men in uniform, likely figures from Mussomeli's history. There were two tufted leather chairs in front of the desk, which had a seal on it like the one on the door. It was all very official and stuffy, and smelled slightly of cigar smoke and furniture polish.

She quickly crept across the thick, royal red carpet to the solid oak desk. Skirting around it, she stared at his empty blotter, just as outside, the band began to play a lively march. She stood there, hand on her chest, trying to control her rapidly beating heart.

What exactly am I looking for here?

The first thing she noticed was that Fanelli was not exactly a techie. His desk was remarkably clear. There was no computer, no laptop, not even an electric typewriter. Instead, at the very head of his desk, next to a cup holding various pens and a gold frame with him next to a smiling, older, blonde-bobbed woman who must be his wife, was a desk calendar, filled with his appointments for the day. Squinting in the darkness, she read:

9:00 AM: Lacardo
10:00 AM: Scarzi
11:00 AM: Parata @ Piazza Grande

11:30 AM: Pranzo @ LMV

Pranzo. Lunch. And *LMV?* What was that?

The answer came to her almost immediately. *La Mela Verde.*

Proud of herself from deciphering that clue, despite it meaning absolutely nothing, she reached forward to flip the page to see what had been on his agenda for the previous day, when Cascarelli died.

A sound of someone shouting outside jolted her. She froze, holding her breath, her heart beating in her ears. She stared at the doorknob, willing it not to turn. It didn't. She let out another sigh of relief and looked back at the page.

Just more meetings. *What did you expect it to say? 10PM – Kill Vito?*

But she needed to get moving. So far, the only thing she'd found out was that the mayor was a fan of G's cooking, too. She needed to find something good. Something damning. Some dirt about the renovations that might tie into why Cascarelli had been murdered.

She leaned over and pulled open one of the drawers, looking for anything of interest. All she found was a stapler, a few paper clips, all the ordinary things a desk would have.

She opened the bottom drawer to find files upon files. Not sure where to start, she glanced through the different tabs. She pulled the first one out and found that it was just a bunch of receipts from some hotel opening in 2012.

Nope, not it. She stuffed it back into the drawer. *Come on, Audrey. Keep looking. What renovation was Cascarelli interfering in? You're on the right trail. I can feel it.*

She scanned the rest of the tabs until she found one marked *piano di sviluppo*. She wasn't sure what it meant, but it was the only tab that was in all caps, which made her think it was important.

She pulled it out, spread it over the blotter, and started to go through a stack of documents, two inches thick. There were papers, contracts, receipts, letters, and blueprints and maps of the town.

Though it was all in Italian, as she paged through it, she started to get a very sick feeling in her stomach. The mayor clearly had big development aspirations for Mussomeli. One of the maps showed quite distinctly a ten-year plan to develop the city into some kind of commercial center of Sicily. She wasn't absolutely sure, but what it looked like was that once the dollar-homes were sold to expats, they'd put up shopping malls and big-box stores that would surely put the little guys out of business. Not only that, it'd totally ruin the character of the town.

These were the big revitalization plans the mayor had in mind for Mussomeli? No wonder Cascarelli had tried to shut them down. She paged through, contract after contract, letter after letter, finding more and more to be sick about. A giant new supermarket. A department store. Three strip malls. A family fun center?

She snorted. "Really? He can't be serious. If I wanted to live in America, I'd have lived there."

Outside, the sounds of the band's upbeat march had faded away. That meant it wouldn't be long before people came back. Grabbing her phone, she spread the map out and took a few pictures of the relevant plans and letters, hoping to decode the rest of it later. Setting her phone down, she went through the rest of the file cabinet, trying to see if there was anything else of interest. Then she closed the folder and stuffed it back into the drawer.

Suddenly, her phone buzzed, making her jump nearly to the ceiling. She glanced at the glowing display to find a message from Mason: *I'm here. Where are you?*

She imagined him sitting outside, waiting for her. Didn't she tell him that she'd left the key? She looked around. If she told him the truth, he'd never believe her. Or he *would* believe her, and insist she see a psychiatrist, and probably wouldn't let her sleep on his sofa anymore.

She opened the door and peered outside. The hallway was still empty. She slipped out and walked away from the door, heaving a breath of relief. When she got to the main lobby, she looked out the revolving doors. The crowd was dissipating, and the mayor was nowhere to be found. He'd probably gone on to his lunch date.

Stepping outside, she typed in: *At city hall. For the parade?*

A moment later, he replied: *Nice that you have time to enjoy yourself. Get your butt over here.*

She frowned. She'd told him no way was she ever going in that dark, spider-filled hole. Couldn't he just handle the repair himself? Yes, it was her clinic, her responsibility … but the most she'd be able to offer him was moral support. Besides, she had other things on her mind right now.

Big things.

She typed in: *Just let yourself in with the key. I'll be there in half an hour,* pocketed her phone, and broke into a run down the staircase, toward La Mela Verde.

CHAPTER TWENTY THREE

Audrey stopped short when she got to the café. *What am I going to do? Go in there and confront him in front of everyone? Accuse him of trying to ruin the town? That's rash and insane, even for me.*

She turned around, ready to head back to the clinic and talk to Mason. She needed to get him to talk her down from the ledge she was dangling from, the one that would probably have her kicked out of the city, if she didn't watch herself.

But she only got a few steps before a black Fiat pulled up in front of the café.

The words Luca had said to her came rushing back to haunt her: *I did see a black car. It go down the street, very slow. Like it was looking for something. I thought that funny. I could not see in. Windows were dark.*

Audrey stared. The windows in this car were tinted so she couldn't see who was driving it.

That is, until the door opened, and out popped the mayor.

Audrey's jaw dropped. So he had been the one slowly making his way down the street by the clinic, casing the joint? That could only mean one thing ...

He was her guy.

As she was trying to come up with a plan, her phone buzzed again. She looked down, annoyed, expecting more questions from Mason. Instead, it was Brina: *I'm assuming you're dead, jerk.*

Brina needed to chill. She'd get to her later. Audrey took a step backward, slinking into an alley, as she watched him and a couple of other men in suits shaking hands in front of the café. He was all smiles, the town-destroying, murdering jerk. He grabbed the door and ushered the other men in.

That does it, she thought, gritting her teeth as she crossed the street to the café. *I don't need Mason to talk me down from any ledge. I'm going full-on psycho on this scumbag.*

She reached for the door, which to her surprise, almost opened into her face as someone came out. "*Scuzi,*" the man said, holding the door open for her. She didn't respond. The place was packed with the lunch rush. She scanned over the heads of the people, looking for the mayor, and found him, in a large, reserved table in the back of the restaurant.

Audrey had only taken one step in that direction when a voice called, "*Principessa!*"

For a second, she wondered if she should ignore it, but then she decided that G deserved to know. Just in case things got ugly and tomato sauce and silverware went flying. It would be good to have someone on her side.

He came around the counter and approached her with his normal greeting, hands on her shoulders, a kiss on each cheek. "Table for one, or can I give you a spot at the bar?"

She shook her head and said, in a low voice, "I'm not here to eat. This isn't a social call. I'm here to—"

"Eh?" He cupped a hand around his ear and leaned forward. "I can't hear you. You must speak up, little *principessa*."

Normally, she loved G's theatrics and ebullient personality, but now, she just wanted to put a lid on it. Her eyes went to the side, where she could see the mayor, opening his menu and saying something to one of his lunch companions. He laughed raucously, unaware of her staring.

"The mayor," she said, a little louder. "I need to speak with him."

G looked over his shoulder. "*Si.* That is the mayor of Mussomeli, Signore Fanelli. What do you need?"

"Do you know him well?"

"I know him as well as I know anyone," he said, nodding.

That means he knows him very well, Audrey thought, since G knew just about everyone well. "What do you think about him?"

He shrugged. "What do you mean, Audrey?"

"I mean, like, is he good? Or is he more ... shady?"

He laughed. "Shady? No. Not at all. He's a good mayor. A good man. I like." He frowned. "What is this all about, Audrey? Is there a problem?"

"Yes. He's a snake, that's what he is," she said, indignant. *Like* him? How? He clearly didn't know all the underhanded things the mayor was up to. "He's planning on turning Mussomeli into America, basically. Did you know that? Forcing little places like yours and all the other mom-and-pop shops in town out of business in favor of big corporate places."

G looked around at the customers nearby, who were starting to take notice of them, since Audrey was so angry, she was shaking. "How do you know this?"

Audrey glared at the mayor, who, still unaware of her, was smiling and laughing like he wasn't the biggest flim-flam artist in history. "I saw it with my own eyes."

"You saw *what*, exactly?"

She didn't want to go into that here, especially now that people were starting to notice her. She shook her head. "It doesn't matter. I just know. He's going to ruin this town as we know it. And I can't sit by and watch it happen."

With that, she sidestepped G. He grabbed for her arm, clearly not wanting her to make a scene, but she shook herself loose, weaving her way through the tables. As she marched up to the table, she heard a man speaking Italian in a stuttering French accent, something about how happy he was to be in such a lovely town for a wonderful celebration. Audrey would've been proud of herself for interpreting the words, but she was fired up, her wrath focused on the mayor.

As if on cue, the heads of all four men swung in her direction.

She opened her mouth to speak, but the mayor beat her to it. *"Vorrei un litro di vino della casa."* I would like a liter of house wine.

She froze there for a beat, completely distracted from her purpose.

Then she gulped a breath and said, in a shrieking voice, *"I am not your waitress!"*

Behind her, the room went completely silent. The mayor looked around, confused. Then he shrugged and motioned her away, as if he had no need for her.

"Listen here, Mayor. I know what you are up to," she said, loudly enough for the other patrons to hear. She'd quieted the room better than a tray of dishes crashing to the floor. But at that moment, she didn't care. These people deserved to know what a creep he was. "I know that you are planning on turning Mussomeli into one big shopping complex."

Near her, someone gasped, which distracted her enough that she looked over her shoulder. Here she was on center stage, with at least fifty people watching her, wondering what she'd do next. The mayor pulled on his collar and looked around helplessly.

"Dear," he said condescendingly. "I have no idea what you're talking about. Could you please leave us to eat in peace?"

132

She fisted her hands on her hips. "No. Not until you answer for what you've done. What you're *planning* to do."

The French businessman's eyes narrowed. "I do not understand. What is this?"

"It's the mayor selling out the citizens of Mussomeli who voted him into office," Audrey said.

The mayor looked about his audience, and his mouth stretched into an uncomfortable smile. "I don't know who you are, girl, but this is not the time nor the place. If you'll make an appointment down at city hall, I'll be happy to—"

"Eh, what kind of shopping center, *Dottore*?" G broke in, standing at her side. "You're speaking of other restaurants that might compete with my place?"

She nodded. "Big ones. Chain restaurants. He basically wants to turn this place into one big shopping district."

More gasps. Waitresses stopped with their heavy trays suspended near their ears. Diners paused mid-bite. Even the clock on the wall seemed to stop ticking and the lively accordion music being piped in through hidden speakers seemed to have screeched off-track. Everyone was absolutely still, hanging on the mayor's next words. The drama unfolding before their eyes was just too good.

"That's absurd. Where are you getting this information?" the mayor sputtered, the fear and doubt now clear in his eyes.

"Let's just say that I've seen the plans with my own eyes."

He coughed. "What did you see? Because yes, plans have crossed my desk, but I have not given a green light to go forward with—"

Suddenly the door swung open, and Officer Ricci and another police officer came in, led by a tiny woman who Audrey kind of recognized, though she couldn't place where. The woman's eyes landed on Audrey and her face brightened with triumph. "There! There she is. The American!"

At that moment, Audrey realized exactly where she'd seen the woman before. It was the lady from the information desk at city hall.

Oh no.

The tiny older lady, who looked very mild-mannered and sweet, what with her glasses on a chain around her neck and her fuzzy pink cardigan, stomped over to Audrey. "Mayor, I saw this woman coming out of your office while you were at the parade."

Audrey winced. Was the information booth in view of his office? Probably. She hadn't noticed that before. Darn.

133

Now, everyone was looking at her, their eyes demanding an explanation.

"Well, yes. I was there," she fudged, her voice barely audible, even in the quiet. "You see, I just knocked because I wanted to speak to you, and—"

"I think she stole something!" the woman shouted.

"*Dottore*. Is that true?" Officer Ricci asked, clearly disappointed in her. "Tell me it is not true."

All those damning expressions focused on her, making her wish she could melt into the floor. "What? No. Of course not. I didn't take a thing. I just ..."

"*Dottore*, maybe you and me go downtown? Talk about this and let these people enjoy their food?"

That's a nice way of saying "you're under arrest for trespassing." Oh, God. Now I really am going to jail.

"No. No, wait." She shook the advancing officers away and grabbed her phone out of her pocket, her hand so slick with sweat that she could barely get it to function. "Look. I'll show you. I have proof that what I said is true."

Even G had been starting to distance himself from her, but now, as she paged through her photographs, he came closer and took the phone from her hands. As she pointed out the photos, she was only partially aware of other people holding their phones up, recording the whole exchange. *If I end up on national news and Brina texts me, I'm going to die.* "Look at that," she said to G. "That's right next to your restaurant."

"Papa D's Spaghetti Warehouse," G said, and his eyes widened. "Is that another restaurant?"

"Yes, it's a big chain from Palermo! Like I said, the whole thing is a plan to make all these crazy shopping malls!" she said desperately, looking over at the mayor, who from his expression, had more than had his lunch ruined by her intrusion. She didn't care. "And what you don't know is that I heard him and the new inspector talking about Vito Cascarelli, the inspector who was killed, and how he was ruining their revitalization plans! Plus—"

"Whoa, whoa, whoa," G said, as the rest of the group erupted.

"Are you accusing me of murder, now, too?" the mayor asked, incredulous.

She'd hoped that Officer Ricci would agree, head over to the mayor, and snap some cuffs on him. That didn't happen. Instead, he just stared at her for a beat. "Maybe he make bad plans for the town, but you have no proof that he committed this murder, Audrey."

"But I do!"

More gasps.

The mayor swept the napkin off his lap and tossed it on the table. "This is absolutely preposterous. I refuse to sit around listening to this rubbish. I'm leaving."

He stood up and took one step, but that was as far as he got.

"Hold it," Officer Ricci said, lifting a finger to him. "*Dottore*, please tell me what you're talking about?"

"Well, it makes sense. He had a black Fiat with dark windows, and there was a black car seen casing my clinic, shortly before the murder. Ask Luca, the boy from the hardware store," she announced. "He witnessed the whole thing. Don't you see, Officer? It all fits together."

The mayor slumped down into his seat as Ricci considered this. "So what? Many people have black cars. What does that mean? It means nothing!"

"You have motive. There was a witness who saw a car fitting your description on the scene," Ricci said. "Where were you that night?"

"That night," the mayor said, stunned. "I don't know. I think I was home."

"And your wife can verify that?"

"Well, yes. Actually, no. That was the night of her weekly ladies' get-together at the school. They make crafts for children in the hospital. And I believe she stayed with her sister that evening. But I wasn't anywhere near—"

"I see."

The other officer took Audrey's phone from G and stared at the plans, then motioned to Ricci, who studied it, a vaguely disgusted expression on his face. "You were going to rip down the park where I play football as a kid? All my life? For a big movie theater?"

The mayor's voice was small now, miserable. "It was just an idea."

Then something happened that Audrey could not believe. Officer Ricci did indeed pull out his cuffs, and motioned to the mayor to give him his wrists.

"I'm under arrest?"

The officer nodded. "*Si*. Charged with the murder of Vito Cascarelli."

More gasps erupted around the place. The mayor's eyes went wide and he blustered, "But I didn't—"

"I'd let your lawyer speak for you, now, *Signore.*"

Reluctantly, the mayor pushed up his sleeves and held his fleshy forearms out to the officer, then glared at Audrey. "Oh, I will. This is ridiculous."

Oh my God, she thought. *I did it again. The mayor of Mussomeli is going to jail for murder.*

She averted his dagger-like eyes as he was led out the door, leaving the rest of the restaurant patrons staring after her.

As she stood there, watching him leave, she waited for the relief to fall over her, that sense that now, everything was right with the world. But for some reason, it didn't. Something tickled in the back of her mind, something she couldn't quite bring to the forefront. Whatever it was, she had the distinct feeling that she'd missed something.

The rest of the restaurant went back to their meals, and business as usual. G rubbed her shoulder and said, "That was exciting, no? I can't believe that the mayor ... after all this, he was a murderer. He was an important man. A good man. A powerful man."

A shiver went down Audrey's spine, because she had to admit that, although she didn't know the mayor well, something about it didn't feel right. *A powerful man who will make my life in Mussomeli a living hell if they ever find out he didn't do it.*

Her phone dinged in her hand. A message from Mason: *I'm leaving.*

She'd noticed a few messages on her phone when she'd tried to show the plan to the police, but she'd quickly cast them aside, unread.

Now she pulled up the messages on her phone to find four others from Mason:

Can I use the sink in the bathroom or do you want me to use the utility sink in the back room?

It's been a half hour. Where are you?

Hello?

Are you alive?

Whoops. She was an hour later than when she'd told him she'd meet him. *On my way,* she typed in.

Waving at G, she said, "Sorry, I have to get back to the clinic," and broke into a run as she pushed her way out of the café and into the afternoon sunshine.

CHAPTER TWENTY FOUR

She arrived to find Mason on the front stoop, paging with one thumb through his phone, drinking a can of soda with the other hand. His face was sweaty and his white T-shirt was stained with sweat and mold. "Well, look who it is. Nice for you to join us."

"Hi," she said. "Sorry. I had some things to—"

"I know. You're a regular media darling, ain't you?"

"What?"

He moved over on the stoop to let her sit and thrust the phone under her nose. Sure enough, there was a grainy video of her, confronting the mayor at La Mela Verde. She winced. "Where did you—"

"It's all over Facebook right now. Making friends in high places, huh, Boston?"

Great. Brina's definitely going to call me tonight when she sees that. She sighed. "Ugh. I didn't mean for it to blow up into this big media circus, but I needed to get in front of him right away, and that was the only way I could do it."

He tilted his head as he watched the video, where Audrey, looking half-insane, thrust an accusing finger at the mayor. "You really broke into his office?"

"*Broke in* is a little harsh. The door was open."

"That being said, did you go someplace where you weren't allowed, which is called trespassing, and is in fact, illegal?"

She smirked at him. "Well. Yes. But ..."

"But Nancy Drew saves the day again. So the murderer's been caught and all your past crimes are forgiven. Is that it?"

"Better to beg forgiveness than ask permission, I guess." She shrugged. "So how's it going with the mold?"

"Getting there. Should have it scrubbed pretty well by tonight, then I'll do a second sweep to get rid of everything I missed the first time. Okay?"

She nodded. This was really great. Everything was working out in her favor. And yet, for some reason she couldn't quite pinpoint, something was off. "Yeah."

He went on, talking about the specific steps he'd taken, and she nodded along, thinking about the case. G had said the mayor was a good man, but G liked everyone. The mayor was kind of a pompous jerk. He'd laughed about Vito Cascarelli's death. And those horrible development plans which would serve no purpose other than to line his pockets? Total jerk.

But that didn't mean he was a murderer.

Plus ... the mayor was the one with the power. If he didn't like the inspector, all he had to do was fire him. Murder? That was a little extreme.

"... and she wanted to lodge a complaint against your treatment of her and her family."

Audrey blinked and looked at him. Last she remembered, he was talking about some Mold-B-Gone stuff that had really done the trick. When had he changed the topic? She'd missed the whole beginning of that. "What? Who?"

"Charlotte. The Spider. She's been living down in your crawl space for months and she's very upset that you don't like her the way you care for all the other creatures in your place. After all the insects she's been keeping out." He grinned. "She's really very pleasant when you get to know her. I could reintroduce you."

Audrey nudged his hard shoulder and scrambled to her feet. "Thanks, but no thanks."

She went inside, to the back room with the animals, avoiding the tarps and other materials that Mason had spread out in the main hallway. Setting her purse down, she got to work, doing her regular check-ups and making sure all the animals were well cared for.

Mason came in and leaned on the door jamb. "So case closed, right? Once you get this place reinspected, you can start rolling again?"

She nodded. "How long do you think it'll be?"

"Like I said, almost done. You can probably get the inspector in tomorrow night."

"Oh. Good. I'll call Dellisanti and tell him to put the clinic on his list," she mumbled, peering in on the bunnies. Now they were much more awake, squirming against each other and moving about. It wouldn't be long before they were running all over the place. They were a bundle full of adorableness, but she couldn't bring herself to smile.

"Hey," Mason said. "Anything wrong?"

She sighed. "Well. I feel bad. What if he didn't do it?"

138

Mason winced. "You're second-guessing yourself now, Nancy Drew? You seemed pretty sure in the video."

"Yes, and I do think the guy's involved up to his ears in some pretty shady stuff. Yes, he wasn't the inspector's biggest fan. But I'm not convinced he'd resort to murder."

Mason hitched a shoulder. "Well, if the police interview him, they'll figure out whether they got enough evidence to hold him. It's not your problem." He pushed away from the wall and began to head for the crawl space. "Though I think I've told you that plenty times before, and you keep wanting to *make* it your problem, for some reason?"

"It *is* my problem if I wind up causing him all this trouble, and he's not our man. Not only would I feel terrible, but he'd probably never forgive me."

"Relax. Let the police take care of it," he said.

Right. Since when have you ever known me to relax? she thought. "Thanks for the advice."

"Okay. I'm gonna tidy up back there and head out. You need anything else from me today?"

She shook her head, still only half-listening to him as she cleaned out the nest for the bunnies, giving them fresh bedding. Her mind was whirring with half-baked thoughts, but she couldn't seem to complete a single one of them.

A moment later, he was there again, though she couldn't remember him ever leaving. He stretched his arms over his head, touching the door transom, and said, "You coming back to the house in a bit?"

"Um ..." She looked up, confused. He'd said it almost as if she belonged there, with him. Almost as if she lived there, instead of just being a guest. It startled her enough to break her from her line of thought. "Oh. Yes. I will. Maybe in an hour?"

"All right. I'm making another one of my momma's specialties. You like okra?"

She shrugged. "I've actually ... never had it."

"You're in luck. You'll have it tonight." He yawned and ran his hands through his mop of hair. "See you."

It was only when he was gone that she realized she hadn't responded. That he was being so nice. Making her dinner? Taking care of her crap around the clinic for free? And here she was, treating him like an afterthought. She'd have to do something nice for him soon.

She stooped down to get some new formula for the bunnies. She found the carton and tried to open it, but her fingers were still wet from washing her hands and kept slipping on the lid. Rather than texting Mason back and relying on his muscles yet again, she tried her other hand. Her teeth. A paper towel. Nothing worked.

"Come on, baby. Come on … Gah!" she cried in frustration, banging it on the side of the counter.

When she did that, two things happened. The carton exploded, sending a wave of white formula spewing in all directions, and she knocked her purse from the counter to the floor. Formula dripped over everything—the cabinets, the sanitized utensils, the counters, and, of course, herself. The front of her shirt was drenched.

She let out a sob and looked down. Formula dribbled down the cabinets, landing on the floor, which was, incidentally, where the entire contents of her purse had spilled out.

"Perfect." There was nothing worse than the spoiled-milk smell of old formula. And now, she and all of her belongings were marinating in it. It wasn't like she could run the contents of her purse through the washing machine. Sighing, she wadded up paper towels, dropped to her knees, and plucked her dripping wallet out of the mess, shaking it a little. "This is not what I need right now."

She went through the mess, picking up her housekeys, her lip gloss, her phone. Setting aside the things that could be saved, she spread out some paper towels on the mess, swirling it all together to sop up the spill.

The pack of tissues, a nearly empty sleeve of gum, a few slips of paper were the casualties. As she swept it all together to pick it up and toss it in the trash, she noticed a business card for a woman named Concetta. Oh, right. The veterinary intern. She hadn't even thought of her since she'd tucked this card away. In another life, it'd have been great to have the extra help, especially from someone who knew what she was doing with animals. But now, any thoughts of that were just impossible.

The clinic was a wreck. A total, non-operating, cash-guzzling mess.

Tucking it away in her wallet, she looked down and noticed another business card among the wreckage. It said, *Eton Scarletto, Commercial Developer.*

She remembered vaguely the meeting with that slick used-car salesman who'd attacked her, wanting her to be a part of that PetSense thing. Like she could just give everything up and submit to corporate ownership.

Actually …

She fell backward onto her butt, thinking about it. If she'd had a corporate sponsor, she probably wouldn't have had to worry about paying out of her own pocket to fix up the mold problem. She probably wouldn't have to scrounge around for supplies, celebrating over a few cans of cat food as a donation. She probably would have money in her wallet, enough to pay for all the repairs she needed for her house.

She had to admit, that sounded nice. An easy way to get back on her feet and start taking this dream of hers in the right direction.

If … if … if …

All she had to do was sell her soul.

Which I'll never, ever do, she thought, picking up the pile of trash and getting ready to toss it away. *I don't care if it's hard. I was hired as a small-town vet. That's how I'm going to stay.*

She stood up and held the garbage over the trash can. It had barely fallen from her fingertips when she noticed something on the business card. *Eton Scarletto.*

E.S.

Where had she seen those initials before? Somewhere very recently. Well, sure, he was probably all over this town, trying to spread his gloomy message of corporate greed. Who knew what other companies he represented? Maybe he'd gone around to dozens of places, offering the opportunity to incorporate.

"Ugh. I hope no one took him up on that offer," she muttered.

When she turned away from the trash can, it hit her like a lightning bolt.

E.S. Of course. Now she knew where she'd seen that.

She scrambled to her wet phone, picking it up in her hand. Now, it was rather sticky, the surface covered with a filmy white liquid. She wadded the bottom hem of her T-shirt and wiped it down quickly, then opened it to the photographs she'd taken earlier that day of the plans she'd seen in the mayor's office. She used her thumb and forefinger to zoom in.

Sure enough, on the very corner of the blueprint, were the initials *ES.*

The blueprints were part of a proposal from Eton Scarletto.

"Oh my god," she whispered, rising to her feet, the half-formed thoughts finally completing in her head. What if Mayor Fanelli had been telling the truth when he'd said those things were just a proposal, and he hadn't yet agreed to them? What if Eton Scarletto had been talking to more businesses, but knew that Cascarelli would never let those changes be made? That figured into the conversation she'd overheard. In fact, as she stood there, staring at the business card, everything seemed to fall into place.

"Well, Audrey, there's only one way to find out for sure," she said aloud.

She grabbed her phone and punched in the numbers on the business card.

CHAPTER TWENTY FIVE

About an hour after she made the call, Audrey sat at the reception desk, a bundle of nerves as she opened the day's mail. As she slipped her finger under the flap of an envelope, pain sliced through it. "Ouch!" she said, watching the blood bubble on the surface of her finger.

Well, it was a lot better than the injury her poor, retired letter opener had been capable of.

She sucked on her finger until the paper cut went away. As she piled up the mail—more bills she wasn't sure how she was going to pay—a text came in from Mason. *On your way home? Food's hot. BBQ chicken and stewed okra with tomatoes.*

She felt a pull in her heart. How adorable was he? She checked the time. She'd said she'd be there by now. Darn.

She started to thumb in a response when the door opened and in walked the used-car salesman himself, Eton Scarletto. He was once again dressed to the nines in an expensive three-piece suit, his abundant dark hair slicked back from his face. He held a shiny leather briefcase. Audrey got the feeling that this was a uniform he never broke from, no matter what the day. But there was something different about him. His eyes were dark-rimmed, and a few shards of that slicked-back hair were falling in his face. Also, he had a tiny stain—mustard, maybe—on his tie.

Guilty conscience? she wondered.

"Mr. Scarletto," she said with a smile. "Thanks for coming by."

"Ah, no problem, no problem at all," he said, looking around the place once again. It was almost as if she could see the dollar signs in his eyes. He let out a grating and awkward guffaw. "I have to admit, I was pretty sure I'd never hear from you in a million years. I thought you'd tossed my business card away."

"Oh. Of course not," she said, even though it had seen the bottom of her trash can not long ago. It was only by sheer luck that she'd actually kept it. She motioned him to follow her. "Come on back. We'll be more comfortable in my office, Mr. Scarletto."

"Please. Call me Eton," he said as they went inside her office. She closed the door behind him. He sniffed. "Uh … is something … spoiled?"

"Oh, no," she said, sitting down at her desk and lacing her hands in front of her, blocking out the terrible milk stain on the front of her shirt. "Just a little unfortunate accident. You know, taking care of animals all day. Please sit."

He sat down, admiring her décor. Since she hadn't been here long, her office lacked all the knickknacks and piles of paper that she'd had at her desk in Boston, but he focused in on her Pet of the Year calendar. "Cute pup. I love dachshunds."

"Hmm," she said, smiling up at the animal, thinking, *Actually, you're only half-right, that's a Chiweenie. But whatever!* She had business to attend to. "I asked you to come in because I might be interested in your proposal. You seemed to have ideas for this place that involved corporate expansion, and I really wanted to hear them. So, please. Tell me your plans."

"Yes, indeed," he said, reaching into his briefcase and fetching an equally spotless leather-bound notebook. He opened it and crossed one leg over the other. "You see, I'm an expat, too, and when I came to this lovely city a little over a year ago, I saw that there was a definite way to capitalize on all the traffic being sent to the city from people taking part in the one-dollar house deal. There's a market that's previously been untapped. And these people are hungry, usually wealthy consumers. They need shopping options similar to the places they came from."

Audrey nodded. *But not at the expense of the character of the town.* "So your plan is to create places that give people a sense of their home, right here in Mussomeli?"

"Yes, essentially. People from away aren't used to going from store to store to get the things they need. They don't have time for that. So my proposal is to create something like PetSense right here in Mussomeli—a one-stop shop for all things pets. And of course, your little clinic here can be the cornerstone of a giant pet paradise. I'm telling you." He rubbed his thumb together with his other fingers. "You're talking a gold mine. Obviously it's a split between you and the parent company, usually ninety-ten, but for all the extra work and headache we'd take off your hands? I think you'll be pleased."

He reached into the folder and pulled out a slick brochure, which he passed over to her. It showed a picture of a smiling business owner in an apron, giving the thumbs-up.

144

"That goes over all the specifics."

She glanced at it, not really reading it, as at her elbow, her phone buzzed. Another text from Mason. *Food's cold. You get what you get.*

Despite the snide, Mason-like comment, she wished he was with her now. And Nick? Where was he? She suppressed a shiver; she'd have to do this alone.

"Looks great," Audrey said. "So, have you been presenting things like this to businesses in other sectors?"

He crossed his fingers in back of his head and gave her a proud grin. "Yep. All over."

"And people have been receptive?"

"Most definitely. Restaurants, supermarkets, gas stations, convenience stores, the hardware store. Really, we're trying to hit just about every sector there is. Bring the modern age to this sleepy little town and get it into the twenty-first century. People are really excited, and all signs are saying this is going to be big. *Huge.*"

Okay, do you think you can lay the butter on any thicker? "You've had a lot of people sign on?"

"Not yet. I'm just beginning, really. But it's good to get in early. You know, get in on the ground floor, so to speak. I've sunk a lot into incentives and advertising and what I've done so far is really causing a buzz. I heard the demand to buy one-dollar houses has never been so high. People want in on a hip, fun Mussomeli. I'd like to think that's my doing." He grinned broadly.

"That's wonderful."

He reached into his briefcase and pulled out a paper, unfolding it to reveal a blueprint that looked remarkably similar to the one she'd seen in the mayor's office. It was a rough drawing of her clinic, but in the plan, it was only a small part of a massive layout that included everything from rows and rows of pet supplies to grooming stations and a pet daycare/hotel.

"Sounds fabulous." *Okay, time to go in for the kill.* She asked casually, "And what did the town inspector think of these plans?"

She almost saw his stomach dropping underneath that buttoned-up blazer. "Uh … the town inspector? What do you mean?"

"You've spoken with him, right?"

"Of course. I've been in close contact with him for months. He knows every phase of my plans."

"That's interesting."

The man leaned forward. "Why is that?"

"Well, he was pretty hard on this place and my house. He refused to pass anything. I'm sure he wouldn't be so happy about such huge changes happening to the town, would he?"

He coughed. "Actually, it's good for the town. Clearing away all this old, faulty architecture. The inspector agreed with me that it was a good possibility, and he was going to think about—"

"Yes, but what about the other inspector? Vito Cascarelli?"

"Cascarelli?" He swallowed. There was definite recognition there.

"Yes. You know, the one who—"

"I never met any Cascarelli," he said, shaking his head. "All I know is Inspector Dellisanti. That's who I've been dealing with. And he's really interested. He and the mayor—"

"The mayor agreed to a plan like this?"

He nodded. "Well, not yet, but he's taking it under advisement and has shown a lot of interest. Once he gives it the okay, then I fully expect to go forward, signing contracts with people like you so we can get this started." He smiled. "So can I put you on the 'interested' list?"

Audrey listened and nodded, all the while turning his words over in her head. He'd been in close contact with the inspector for months, and yet he never met Cascarelli, who'd only died a few days ago? That made no sense.

It's him. Of course. He's the killer.

And now, it was getting dark, shadows were closing in, and it seemed like the walls of the building were, too. Suffocating her.

"Are you all right?" he asked, that smile that had once seemed to be tattooed on suddenly fading.

"Ye-es," Audrey said unconvincingly, her voice cracking. She scanned her desk and focused on her personal letter opener, wondering if it would be too obvious if she reached out and grabbed it.

He seemed to notice it at the exact same time, and his brows tented. "Are you sure, Dr. Smart?"

A sick feeling overcame her. The person who had killed Vito Cascarelli hadn't poisoned him or pushed him. He'd done something particularly evil, something unspeakably vile. He'd attacked him with a sharp instrument, plunged it into his throat, letting him bleed out as he watched. She couldn't help but think it took a special kind of monster to do such a thing, a cold, calculating individual who would stop at nothing to carry out his plans.

A monster like the man sitting in front of her.

And she was all alone with him.

Right then, something G had said suddenly stuck in her mind. *If a man commits murder, there is little to stop him from murdering again to conceal the first crime. You could be in danger. Yes?*

Her heart thudded in her chest.

Yes. Most definitely.

CHAPTER TWENTY SIX

The second Audrey picked up her phone, Eton Scarletto leaned forward. "What are you doing?"

She started to type in a message to Mason. "Ah, my uh—boyfriend is just wondering where I am. He made me dinner," she said, her fingers moving feverishly. *Help me.* "Just typing in a message for—"

Before she could press the send button, he swept across the desk and grabbed the phone from her. The sound of the struggle was so loud, the animals in the other room began to go crazy, barking and yipping.

She swiped for it, panic rising up inside her. "Hey. What are you—"

He checked the display. His voice was unusually low and not salesman-like in the least. "Help you?" He let out a bitter laugh and slipped the phone into his own pocket. "No one can help you."

At that moment, she had the feeling he was right. Never had she felt so alone.

"What—what do you mean? What are you doing? Give me my phone back," she said, staring at the letter opener. It was at the other side of her desk, closer to him. He could easily just pick it up and then it would be all over.

He smiled. "I don't think so." He laughed again. "So, what? Why'd you bring me here? You knew Cascarelli? Were you trying to trap me?"

"What did you do?" she asked, voice shaking, standing up and moving behind her office chair just to get away from him, in the chance he might lunge at her.

"What do you think? I got into this business because I don't let anyone stop me. That's why I'm successful. And I'm not going to let some second-rate, minimum-wage inspector put the brakes on my plans for expansion. He wanted to, yes. He thought he had my number. But he didn't. And neither do you."

Audrey whispered, "You killed him."

"Of course. With the plans I have, people like him are nothing. Dust. They mean absolutely nothing in the grand scheme of things." He reached into the cup on her desk and ever so slowly pulled out the letter opener. Gleaming in the fluorescent light overhead, it looked sharper than Audrey remembered. She froze in fear as she stared at it, her eyes widening. "I could tell, you know, that you were going to be as big a problem as he was. That of everyone, you'd hold out and foul things up. So when I caught up with him, right here at the clinic, and found the door open? It was serendipity. I'd heard the clinic had failed inspection, which was no surprise. I thought I could kill him, blame it on you. Two birds, one stone. Easy as pie.

"But then the police didn't arrest you. Stupid flatfoots in this town, don't know how to conduct a proper investigation. So when you called, I figured this was my chance at making everything right."

He smiled.

"You don't have to ..."

"Oh, yes I do. You think you're going to stop me? Have me fall on my knees and beg for forgiveness? No. I've made my plans. And with you out of the way, the sky's the limit, baby."

She backed up against the wall, staring at the gleaming letter opener, her heart in her throat. "You're going to stab me?"

"Actually, no," he said, reaching into his briefcase. From it, he pulled a small amber vial and a syringe. "This, here, I'm sure you're familiar with. I had to go through one of your competitors to get it, but I know you will understand."

"What is it?" she asked, barely able to speak the words. It didn't matter. She had a very good idea of what it was.

"It's pentobarbital, which, from what I hear, is the main drug used in animal euthanasia. I'm sure you've used it before?" He raised an eyebrow at her.

Yes. Of course, any veterinarian had, for the unpleasant act of putting an animal to sleep. Enough of it would stop the heart of a creature in mere minutes. She hugged herself and moved into the corner, flattening herself there.

He smiled. "I hear it's also used in human euthanasia, too. So correct me if I'm wrong, but it would be an effective and readily available tool, in case a veterinarian wanted to end it all? I mean, I heard of your little brush-up with the mayor. In fact, everyone in Sicily has. You looked a bit ... shall we say, unhinged? Crazy? Apt to go to extremes?"

She couldn't deny that. She'd seen the video, too, and that wild look in her eye. "Yes, but no one would believe—"

149

"I think they will. Imagine the headlines. *Doctor Commits Suicide Over Implicating Wrong Man in Murder She Committed.* It happens. You just got tired of piling up lie after lie in your quest to cover the truth—that you were the one who murdered Vito Cascarelli. You couldn't take the guilt, and you just snapped. Luckily, you had the drugs on hand."

"You're not going to get away with this," she said, knowing it was a cliché. And totally wrong. Because, right now, she didn't see any way he *wouldn't* get away with this. He was by the door. Her back was against the wall. There was nowhere to go. All he had to do was prick her with that needle, she'd go down in infamy as a murderer, and no one would question it.

Would they? Maybe Mason would. G, possibly. But without evidence, they'd let it go. They didn't have her tenacity, her inability to back down when it came to uncovering the truth.

Oh, why oh why are you so tenacious, Audrey? Why can't you ever let anything go?

He simply laughed, as if he knew she was done for. He knew he had her. He knew her situation was hopeless. If he'd so easily stab Vito Cascarelli to death, there was nothing to prevent him from pricking her with that needle to cover it up. She stared at it, wide-eyed, as he opened the cap of the vial, depressed the plunger, stuck it in the vial, and gradually let the syringe fill with the barbiturate.

The best I can do is hope to stall him, she thought. "All right. I guess you have me," she said, trying to think fast. "So ... when I'm dead, are you going to turn this place into a PetSense?"

He looked around, and as he did, she scanned the area, too, trying to find something to use as a weapon. The only thing nearby was the sweater she'd draped over the back of her chair, to ward off the chill that seemed to gather in her office from the air conditioning ... and the chair itself. Not exactly helpful. "Probably. It's a hole, really. But with enough money and luck, it could be pretty decent. Although, I guess we'll have to get another veterinarian in, because you won't be here to see it."

Face twisted in a wolfish sneer, he started to walk toward her, sidestepping around her desk, the syringe poised and ready to insert.

When he got a few steps from her, she grabbed the chair and shoved it with all her might.

It was exactly as much help in deterring him as she'd thought. He simply grabbed ahold of it and wheeled it out of the way. She reached

150

forward for it, trying to keep it between them as a barrier, but he shoved it behind him, so that the only thing left in her hands was her cardigan. Balling it up, she tossed it at him and attempted to climb over the desk, to freedom.

Another pathetic attempt. He easily swatted it away and lunged before she could get too far.

She tried to scream as he grabbed ahold of her arm, but all that came out was a frightened squeak as he locked his hand around her wrist. As he pinned her to the desk, she reached for something, anything. Struggling as he tried to find a place to insert the needle, she grabbed the pen cup, the tissue box on the top of her desk, and hurled them at him. They bounced off him as he continued, undaunted. "Stop squirming," he growled, trying to hold her arm still.

His body had her entire lower half wedged against the desk. She'd just freed her leg, ready to kick him in the crotch, when she heard the unmistakable sound of footsteps in the hallway outside.

A voice said, "You know, Boston, sometimes I think you live to make my life a living—"

At that moment, Mason appeared in the doorway.

The next few moments seemed to happen in slow motion. Eton Scarletto, his concentration broken, pushed the syringe closer. Audrey latched a hand around his wrist, trying to shove him back. The needle moved ever closer to the crook of her arm.

And her foot jammed into his crotch. He let out a guttural "oof" and went reeling backward, reaching for his privates.

She saw Mason's face morph from confusion, to anger, to absolute shock before he finally comprehended the scene developing in front of him and bridged the distance. "What the—? Get off her!"

Face red with rage, Eton Scarletto spun away from Audrey, came around the desk, and lunged at him, shoving him back against the wall and pinning him there.

"Mason!" she shouted. "Stay away from the syringe!"

It was almost too late. The syringe came within inches of Mason's neck before he grabbed Eton's wrist. The two engaged in a power struggle, the syringe hovering between them, poised just inches away from Mason's carotid artery.

Grabbing the first thing she could find, her tissue box, Audrey scuttled over the desk and whacked Eton over the head with it.

It stunned him just enough to allow Mason to push him away.

The commotion was enough to get the animals in the back room riled. Choruses of howls and excited barks filled the air.

Eton, still stunned, took a half-hearted step forward to make another attack, then paused to take the two of them in. In a split second, he dropped the syringe and took off running, headed for the back room.

In a heartbeat, Mason pushed off the wall and tore after him. At his heels were Polpetto and Nick.

Audrey went into the hallway in time to see Mason disappearing out the back door, as well as nearly a dozen of her strays. How had they gotten loose?

She followed along, struggling to follow the last dog. They were far too fast for her. She came to the end of the drive and by the time she got there, they'd disappeared out of sight. She had to follow the sound of their excited yips and barks. Out of breath, she stopped a couple times due to the stitch in her side, but after a few moments, when she turned a corner, she found all the dogs on Scarletto's heels. She was just in time to witness them all jumping on his back as a team, pinning the man to the ground.

Mason dragged him up by the collar of his jacket. "What do you think you were doing?" he demanded.

As Audrey approached, she panted, "He's the one. He killed the inspector. And he was going to try to kill me with the syringe of pentobarbital and make it look like a suicide."

"Pento-what?" Mason growled, shoving him up against the brick side of a building.

"Forget it," she said, the adrenaline inside her slowly dissipating, her heartbeat gradually returning to its normal pace. She didn't have her phone, so she reached into the back pocket of his jeans and pulled his out. "I'm calling the police."

"Yeah. You hear that?" Mason hadn't loosened his grip on the man at all. He jiggled him around for good measure, exuding testosterone. "You're going to prison, scumbag. For a long time."

"Thanks, Mason," she said with a relieved sigh as the phone rang in her ear. "But this isn't *Dragnet*."

CHAPTER TWENTY SEVEN

The police arrived a few moments later. DiNardo hopped out of his squad car as Mason and Audrey took turns explaining what had happened.

As two officers went to put the culprit in cuffs, DiNardo said, "So the mayor didn't do it?" looking right at her.

She shrugged and said in a small voice, "Well, I may have been wrong about that ..."

DiNardo already had his phone at his ear, calling the precinct.

After the excitement simmered down, Audrey called Brina, who answered on the first ring. "Well?"

"Sorry. I've been busy. Catching murderers and stuff."

"Are you kidding me?"

"No, I'm not. I found a guy murdered in my reception area yesterday. And I've been running around since then. But it's all cleared up now." *I think.*

"Really? Who did it?"

"A developer. I think he was getting in the way of his development plans."

"Wow. That's wild. I can't believe it! And here I thought nothing you could tell me would be more exciting than Abs. That almost qualifies."

Audrey laughed. "Oh, well, about Abs. I've been thinking, and—"

She stopped when she looked up and saw him, on the other side of the curb, staring at her. If it hadn't been for him, there was no doubt in her mind that she would be dead. And this was by no means the first time that he'd stuck his neck out for her, saved her. Her heart fluttered at the thought. He quickly averted his eyes and made like he wasn't listening in on her conversation, but there was no doubt about it. He was.

"What?" Brina blared in her ear. "You've realized you need to profess your undying love for him because he's the man of your dreams?"

She swallowed. "Um. I'll talk to you later."

153

She quickly ended the call and went over to him. Before she could say a word, he said, "You talking to your sister about me again?"

She shrugged. "Maybe. A little. She was just saying that the murder was almost as exciting as those selfies you've sent her."

"Ah."

"Thank you for coming when you did. I'm sorry I ruined your dinner," she added.

He hitched a shoulder, his blue eyes locked on hers. "Not ruined. All we need to do is heat it up." He motioned to the animals. "What do you say we get these dogs back where they belong and go eat?"

She nodded, smiling, and was about to follow him back to the clinic when DiNardo held up a hand at her.

"Audrey," he said, pulling the phone from his ear. "The mayor's being released from jail as we speak. And he'd like a word with you, first thing tomorrow morning. His office."

Audrey's stomach dropped.

*

The following day, Audrey sat at one of the chairs in the hallway of city hall, chewing on her fingernails.

Mason grabbed her hand and pushed it away from her mouth before she could gnaw her own fingers off. "Easy."

"Ha. Easy for you to say. You're not about to get your butt handed to you by a man you accused of murder."

He smirked. "Oh, right. That was pretty stupid of you, wasn't it?"

"Ha. Ha."

"Look. Don't forget. The mayor's not an innocent, either. Right? Based on what you heard, he still has plans to turn Mussomeli into one big shopping mall. And that ain't right."

She nodded.

"Not that him being a jerk makes up for you accusing him of murder. If you did that to me, I'd hog-tie you and toss you in jail to rot."

She looked over at him. "You would?"

"Oh, yeah. Maybe he will. Then I can have my sofa back."

She tried to bring her other hand up to her mouth, but he quickly grabbed that one. And he held it tight, entwining his fingers with hers.

She stared at it, a little thrill passing through her. If anyone came by at that moment, they'd have thought they were *together*. Someone *did*

154

come by, and Mason didn't drop her hand, trying to protect whatever lone-wolf image he might've ahead. Instead, he seemed quite comfortable that way. *Happy*, even.

Audrey was so shocked by the move and what it could mean that she actually did manage to forget the mayor and her upcoming punishment for a few moments. But then the door opened, and the short old lady from the information desk, the one who'd caught Audrey doing her little spy routine, came out, a pinched expression on her already-wrinkled face.

"Dottore Smart? The mayor will see you now."

Audrey slowly untangled her hand from Mason's and rose to her feet. She looked down at him for the confidence she sorely lacked. He gave her a thumbs-up and murmured, "Just get it over with."

Right. Butt-kickings didn't last forever. Hopefully, whatever punishment he doled out wouldn't leave any major scars.

"Want me to come in with you?"

"No." *Yes.* But she was an adult. She'd gotten into this mess on her own; she needed to face the consequences on her own, too.

She had to physically concentrate on putting one foot in front of the other, taking the path into the mayor's office. They seemed to have a mind of their own, wanting to rush her toward the nearest exit and carry her out of Mussomeli forever. Her heart pounding and blood swishing in her ears, she passed through the doorway to find the mayor sitting there in his suit, scribbling something on a piece of paper.

He barely looked up as he said, "Take a seat, Dottore Smart."

As if there were a bomb in the office, about to go off, Audrey crept quietly in and sat at the very edge of the tufted leather chair across from the mayor.

He seemed to take his time writing whatever he was writing, paying no mind to her. It was almost as if he wanted to make her wait, to make her dangle in the wind until she could take the torture no longer. She wiped her sweaty hands on her thighs and waited … and waited … until she was about to explode.

That was when he stopped writing and looked up. "Now. Dottore Smart. I don't think I have to explain to you why I asked you over here."

She shook her head. "You don't. And I apologize for blaming the murder of the inspector on you when I clearly didn't know for sure."

"I didn't call you here to apologize to me."

155

"Good. Because I won't apologize for what you're trying to do to the town. If you think you can turn Mussomeli into a strip mall and that the citizens of this town won't fight you tooth and nail, you're sadly mistaken. We moved here to escape all that, and—"

"I wasn't planning on doing that," he said, lacing his fingers in front of him.

"You … weren't?"

"That man I was meeting with? The Frenchman? He was another one with plans to develop the town. I took him out to lunch to tell him that by no means do I agree with those plans. Mussomeli, its people, and its heritage are not for sale."

Audrey's eyes bulged. "What? But I heard you and Dellisanti speaking about revitalization plans. I thought you meant—"

"Yes. The revitalization plans are to enhance the character of the main square. The fountain's crumbling and many of the pathways are shifting and dangerous, causing people to trip. Cascarelli did an in-depth study on the main area and deemed it safe, but we were hoping that he'd look closer into the structure and say it wasn't, because we would really like to use some of our city funds to rehabilitate it. We can't use them, though, until the area has been condemned. That's all."

Audrey didn't speak for a long time, but when she did, her voice was small. "Oh. That's nice."

"Well, it all worked out anyway. The funds have been earmarked now and the fountain area will be revitalized."

"Oh. That's nice," she repeated.

"After I got out of *jail*, I signed the order to make sure that happens." He gave her a deep, meaningful look.

She looked away. "Anyway, I wanted to let you know I grew up here. I care about this town and won't let anyone see it destroyed. That's why I'm being extra careful about the one-euro houses and making sure they go to people who will fix them up appropriately and breathe a life into the community that respects our traditions and culture. And why I was hard on Cascarelli to make sure that the renovations are done right. Perhaps I was too hard, but in my opinion, our city is worth it."

Yes, he was a politician, probably used to saying things to get a vote. But Audrey saw sincerity in his eyes. "That's … wonderful."

"Good. Now that that's settled …" He peered around his desk, shuffling papers around, looking for something. "Now … what did I do with …"

156

She winced. *Probably an order to get out and never show my face in this city again.*

"Ah. Here." He held the paper in front of him, reading it over to make sure it was in order. "I understand you took a risk yesterday, and I'd be remiss if I didn't do this."

Still bracing herself, she looked down.

"We're enormously grateful for what you did to track down Cascarelli's killer," he said.

She looked up. That certainly wasn't the butt-kicking she'd been expecting. In fact, that sounded like a... a compliment? "What?"

He pushed the paper over to her. "So here you go."

She took the papers and stared at them. They were the new certificates of occupancy for her clinic, and her home. "You mean I can …"

"Yes. We'd like you to reopen right away. In case you didn't notice, the town needs a vet." He smiled.

"Well, that's me!" she said, standing up. "I'll get right on it. Everything's almost ready to go. Thank you. I'm going to go there now and—"

"First, I want to discuss something with you."

Audrey stared, her emotions whirling like a tornado inside her now. She'd gone from fear, to elation, to fear, to elation too many times … now, she was starting to feel exhausted. "Yes?"

"A business proposition, if you will."

This sounded an awful lot like Eton's lead-in. "You don't want to make my place into a PetSense, do you?"

He chuckled. "No. But I do want to discuss expanding. I hear the place is quite small and is already at capacity. The building next door is vacant. Do you think you could use the room?"

"Absolutely!" She nodded so much, it was a surprise to her that her head didn't fall off and roll across the room. "I definitely could. But that would require more funds, and more time to—"

"Yes. Well, we'll work out the details. I've also batted around the possibility of hiring an Animal Control Officer to help you out. But we can discuss all this later. You have things to do now. Just go," he said, waving her off.

She rushed out the door and almost forgot about Mason waiting for her. When she ran past him at the door, he had to jog to keep up with her. "Hey. What happened?"

157

"Oh. Look." She held the papers up so he could see them. "I have my new certificates of occupancy. That means that I can open the clinic right away. As soon as you finish with that last treatment. It's almost done, right?"

"Yep. I'm on it. Almost done." He walked in step with her as she pushed open the door and hurried down the steps. "Where you going to now?"

She gave him an incredulous look. Like he even needed to ask that? "Where do you think? The clinic! Being closed for the week, everything's behind. The place is a mess. I have so much to do right now if I want to get it ready to open as soon as possible. Plus, I have to take care of all the animals."

"All right. I'll go with you." Usually, it was Audrey who had to rush to keep in step with Mason, but now he was the one lagging behind. "So ... what did the mayor say?"

"Would you believe, he said that he was never planning on turning Mussomeli into a giant strip mall. I must've misunderstood. Probably because of the language barrier. But all he wanted to do was rehabilitate the town square, which is starting to crumble a little," she said, starting to pant because she was walking so fast down the street and talking even faster. "Anyway, he actually *thanked* me for finding Cascarelli's killer. Can you believe that?"

"Yep."

"And you'll never believe this, but the mayor said something about expanding into the next building. Hiring an Animal Control Officer. Isn't that crazy?"

"No. Not at all. After all the good you've done in this town, Boston, I'm surprised they don't name the whole city after you."

She laughed. "Oh, maybe not the city. But I'd take a street! A little one, maybe on the outskirts of ..."

They'd rounded the corner and were heading down via Barcellona, toward the clinic. She stopped when she got within sight of the door. Sure enough, it was open a crack.

Now, she couldn't blame Luca. She'd been the last person out the door last night, after Eton Scarletto was arrested and everything with the police had been settled. Yes, she'd been exhausted, but had she been so exhausted that she'd left the door open? After what she'd been through ... she pushed open the door, wincing, half-expecting to see another dead body sprawled out on the floor.

Instead, there were a number of bodies there. None dead, thank goodness. All people she'd met before ... Roberto, Dom, and even Horst. Roberto and Dom were working on waxing the floors and Horst was carrying a bucket of dirty water out to the front. They all shouted a hello to her at once, smiling big as she stepped inside, careful not to mess their work, a little shell-shocked at the whole scene.

She looked back at Mason, who was grinning slyly. "What's going ..."

"I knew you were going to need help to open, so I called around and got people here to help finish straightening things up."

"Are you serious?"

"We even walked the dogs, too!" Roberto said. He sat back on his haunches and stroked a very pleased-looking Bruno, who seemed to be supervising the whole job. "Tell me this one is up for adoption?"

"He is. He is one of the best. I can get you an application when we op—"

"You can open tomorrow, if you want. Heck, now, if you really want to," Mason said.

"I can?" She clasped her hands together.

"Why not? You said it yourself. You're untouchable. The mayor *loves* you."

She smacked his arm, then tiptoed around the work and grabbed an adoption application from the stack of papers at reception. As she sat down to fill her part out, she looked up at Mason. "You *knew* the mayor was going to allow me to reopen," she accused.

"I didn't," he said with an innocent shrug. "I just figured you'd been pretty stressed and could use the break."

She smiled. "Thank you," she said, staring at him. He looked back at her, and she felt all warm and gooey inside.

It was what the romance books called "sharing a moment." No, she wasn't Brina, wasn't experienced with men in the least, but at least she could tell that.

CHAPTER TWENTY EIGHT

Montagnanera.

Audrey sat at the reception desk, gazing at the mountains she'd just Googled.

Montagnanera. It meant Black Mountains, which was a perfect name for the place she'd seen in the postcard. Incredibly, it wasn't far away, in the north of Italy, on the Mediterranean Sea. Though the postcard had been taken at sunset, the photos she looked at now were during the day, showing whimsical, brightly colored buildings in the warm sun, cobblestone streets, quaint cafes. She had to smile at that.

It was so similar to the things that had drawn her to Mussomeli.

And it was close.

As if her father had been calling to her all this time.

It was after eight, and she could now call her first day back at the clinic an unmitigated success. Yes, it had been busy, but it felt so good to be back. Even the animals seemed happier to have her around more often. She loved this, and couldn't wait to get back into her groove.

Of course, now it was probably time to go home.

Home. She'd moved her stuff out of Mason's place last night. Thank goodness, she wouldn't have to worry anymore about Polpetto and Nick playing Tom and Jerry, circling each other like opponents ready to battle to the death. Plus, her home was *hers*. She had Horst coming over to help her patch the hole in the floor that weekend.

Things were definitely looking up.

But for some reason, something she couldn't quite put her finger on, she'd been really sad, sleeping in her bedroom, last night. It wasn't just that she loved having Mason cook her dinner when she got done with work, or that it was nice to know he was nearby in case she had a particularly stubborn jar that needed opening, or that he knew how to get rid of black mold. Yes, it was all those things ... but there was something more.

As she sat there, lost in those thoughts and scrolling through the lovely photographs of the high black mountains, covered in snow, the phone in reception began to ring. It'd been ringing off the hook all day, with people wanting to book appointments. She answered. "Hello, Dr. Smart's office."

"Hello. Is this Doctor Smart?"

"Yes."

"Hi. This is Concetta Busillo. I'm a veterinary student. I'm not sure you remember me, but I spoke to you—"

"Yes, actually, I do! Nice to hear from you. And it's so great you're calling! Were your ears ringing? Because I wanted to call you!"

"Oh. You did?"

"Yes!" That wasn't buttering her up. Now that things were moving on, she was ready to hire an intern. The only problem was that the formula spill had completely smeared the ink on Concetta's card, making it impossible to read her phone number. She'd tried to locate her by asking around, but had come up empty. Funny, in a small town, she'd thought it'd be easy to locate a veterinary student, but all of her searches had turned up nothing. "I reopened the clinic today, and I was swamped. I really could use an intern to help me out."

"You could?" There was excitement in the woman's voice. It was kind of cute. "Well, that's me! I'm happy to help! Do you need me to provide a resume or—"

"No. I don't need anything. Just you, to show up here tomorrow morning. Say, eight-thirty? I can show you around the place and get you acquainted before we open. Sound good?"

"Oh, yes! I will be there. *Grazie*, Dottore Smart. I won't let you down."

"I know. See you soon."

She hung up and took one long, last look at those mountains. Could she go to that place? Find him? What would he say to her if she suddenly showed up on his doorstep? Would he be happy? Or would he want nothing to do with her?

She yawned. It was too late to think of such big questions. *One thing at a time is all we can do.*

As she tried to close out the window, an ad popped up. It was the same photograph of those black mountains in the distance, with the headline: *Discount flights to Montagnanera from Palermo! Only $99! Limited Time!*

She clicked on it. The tickets were open-ended. She could buy one now and take a flight anytime she wanted. Take a flight to explore the mountains, enjoy the mainland, maybe even … find her father?

Her breathing shuddered as she pressed on the BUY NOW button. A minute later, she'd entered in her credit card information. Now, she was the proud owner of a round-trip fare to Montagnanera.

Leaving … who knew when. But somehow, it settled her, making her feel closer to whatever destination she'd been on this journey for.

And now, it was time to go home. Back to *her* home.

Her cold, empty home, where she'd have to scrounge together some dinner.

She flipped off her computer, turned out the lights, went outside, and smiled at Nick, who'd come in from his adventures and was now waiting for her, as usual. "Come on, boy. Let's go home. You wouldn't want to cook me dinner, would you?"

No answer.

She sighed as she locked the door up tight. "I didn't think so. Maybe it's time for some *maccu di fave* from Pepe. What do you think, bub?"

Again, no answer, but her stomach seemed to growl in appreciation, which was all the encouragement she needed.

She walked down the street, in the direction of the newly set sun, imagining her father fixing up a house at the base of those lovely black mountains. She imagined him smiling at her, handing her the hammer and asking for her help, like he used to.

Just a pipe dream, she thought, shivering in the chilly air of the night. *Plus, you have so much going on here. Your life is so full. You don't need to worry about a father who abandoned you. Not now that you have …*

Even the thought of noshing on her lovely soup from Pepe didn't seem to settle her. She approached Piazza Tre and something twisted inside her. It looked cold and dark, like no one lived there. Mason's house had been so warm. So welcoming. Every light blazed in the place, and when she was there with him, it felt comfortable. It felt like home.

A feeling suddenly shook her. *You're silly, Audrey. It wasn't the place. It was the person.*

She paused in the street at the realization, and Nick paused too, looking at her curiously. Mason had been there for her through everything. He made her dinners. He held her hand. He put up with all her crazy antics. She'd been ping-ponging back and forth between G and Mason, but if she had to be really honest with herself, there was no contest.

It had been Mason, all along.

Now, she was more certain than ever. In fact, she wanted to scream it from the rooftops. *I love Mason Legare ... and I think he loves me, too.*

Thinking back, it seemed so obvious. There was love in everything he'd done for her. *No, I KNOW it.*

With that thought firmly in her head, she rushed off, so fast that even Nick had trouble keeping up with her. She dashed past her house at the corner of the piazza, down another drive, to via Milano, and didn't stop until she arrived at Mason's front door. As usual, the place was awash in light.

And it felt so right to be standing there, in front of his place, and to finally pour out all the emotions she'd been keeping inside. She took all three steps in one leap and, heart thudding a beat for every one of the possibilities, knocked on the door.

NOW AVAILABLE!

A VILLA IN SICILY: CAPERS AND A CALAMITY
(A Cats and Dogs Cozy Mystery—Book 4)

"Very entertaining. Highly recommended for the permanent library of any reader who appreciates a well-written mystery with twists and an intelligent plot. You will not be disappointed. Excellent way to spend a cold weekend!"
--Books and Movie Reviews (regarding *Murder in the Manor*)

A VILLA IN SICILY: CAPERS AND A CALAMITY is book #4 in a charming new cozy mystery series by bestselling author Fiona Grace, author of *Murder in the Manor*, a #1 Bestseller with over 100 five-star reviews (and a free download)!

Audrey Smart, 34, has made a major life change, walking away from her life as a vet (and from a string of failed romances) and moving to Sicily to buy a $1 home—and embark on a mandatory renovation she knows nothing about. She finds herself busy running the town's new shelter, while also renovating her own problematic home—and dating again.

Audrey's reputation is spreading, and she is asked to travel to other parts of Sicily to help other towns with their animal problems. When she journeys a short ferry ride away to the beautiful Aeolian Islands, Audrey thinks she has found paradise— until a rival vet makes her life hell—and an unexpected murder pins her as the main suspect.

Can Audrey clear her name, salvage her reputation, and find the true killer?

A laugh-out-loud cozy packed with mystery, intrigue, renovation, animals, food, wine—and of course, love—A VILLA IN SICILY will capture your heart and keep you glued to the very last page.

Fiona Grace

Fiona Grace is author of the LACEY DOYLE COZY MYSTERY series, comprising nine books (and counting); of the TUSCAN VINEYARD COZY MYSTERY series, comprising six books (and counting); of the DUBIOUS WITCH COZY MYSTERY series, comprising three books (and counting); of the BEACHFRONT BAKERY COZY MYSTERY series, comprising six books (and counting); and of the CATS AND DOGS COZY MYSTERY series, comprising six books.

Fiona would love to hear from you, so please visit www.fionagraceauthor.com to receive free ebooks, hear the latest news, and stay in touch.

BOOKS BY FIONA GRACE

LACEY DOYLE COZY MYSTERY
MURDER IN THE MANOR (Book#1)
DEATH AND A DOG (Book #2)
CRIME IN THE CAFE (Book #3)
VEXED ON A VISIT (Book #4)
KILLED WITH A KISS (Book #5)
PERISHED BY A PAINTING (Book #6)
SILENCED BY A SPELL (Book #7)
FRAMED BY A FORGERY (Book #8)
CATASTROPHE IN A CLOISTER (Book #9)

TUSCAN VINEYARD COZY MYSTERY
AGED FOR MURDER (Book #1)
AGED FOR DEATH (Book #2)
AGED FOR MAYHEM (Book #3)
AGED FOR SEDUCTION (Book #4)
AGED FOR VENGEANCE (Book #5)
AGED FOR ACRIMONY (Book #6)

DUBIOUS WITCH COZY MYSTERY
SKEPTIC IN SALEM: AN EPISODE OF MURDER (Book #1)
SKEPTIC IN SALEM: AN EPISODE OF CRIME (Book #2)
SKEPTIC IN SALEM: AN EPISODE OF DEATH (Book #3)

BEACHFRONT BAKERY COZY MYSTERY
BEACHFRONT BAKERY: A KILLER CUPCAKE (Book #1)
BEACHFRONT BAKERY: A MURDEROUS MACARON (Book #2)
BEACHFRONT BAKERY: A PERILOUS CAKE POP (Book #3)
BEACHFRONT BAKERY: A DEADLY DANISH (Book #4)
BEACHFRONT BAKERY: A TREACHEROUS TART (Book #5)
BEACHFRONT BAKERY: A CALAMITOUS COOKIE (Book #6)

CATS AND DOGS COZY MYSTERY
A VILLA IN SICILY: OLIVE OIL AND MURDER (Book #1)
A VILLA IN SICILY: FIGS AND A CADAVER (Book #2)
A VILLA IN SICILY: VINO AND DEATH (Book #3)

Printed in Great Britain
by Amazon

36696114R00096